Frightful's Mountain

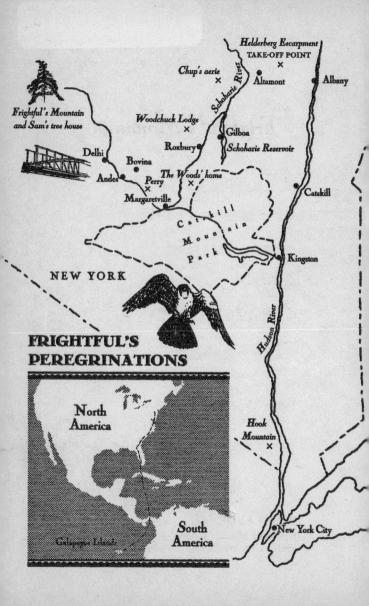

Frightful's Mountain

written and illustrated by

JEAN
CRAIGHEAD
GEORGE

With a Foreword by
Robert F. Kennedy, Jr.

SCHOLASTIC INC.
New York Toronto London Auckland Sydney
Mexico City New Delhi Hong Kong Buenos Aires

ISBN 0-439-20911-0

12 11 10 9 8 7 6 5 4 3 2 1   1 2 3 4 5 6/0

Printed in the U.S.A.   01

First Scholastic paperback printing, September 2001

Designed by Sara Reynolds

To Frank and John

Contents

FOREWORD   ix

FRIGHTFUL TAKES OFF   5

FRIGHTFUL GOES TO FALCON SCHOOL   20

THE EYASES GET ON WING   32

THE WILDERNESS TESTS THE EYASES   42

FRIGHTFUL PEREGRINATES   50

FRIGHTFUL FINDS THE ENEMY   62

DISASTER LEADS TO SURVIVAL   69

HUNGER IS FRIGHTFUL'S TEACHER   82

FRIGHTFUL FINDS SAM   92

THERE ARE EGGS AND TROUBLE   112

THE KIDS ARE HEARD   123

THERE ARE THREE   136

SAM TAKES CHARGE   151

SAM BATTLES BIRD INSTINCTS   160

A PAL FINDS A PAL   172

FRIGHTFUL AND OKSI RUN THE SHOW   195

FRIGHTFUL FEELS THE CALL TO THE SKY   211

THE EARTH CALLS FRIGHTFUL   226

DESTINY IS ON WING   245

AFTERWORD   257

Foreword

In 1986, I met Jean Craighead George at a friend's home in the upstate New York town where we all live. I grew up admiring the Craigheads, a family of naturalists, whose adventures I followed in *National Geographic* magazine, where they always seemed to be attaching transmitters to grizzly bears, banding bald eagles, or paddling canoes and fiberglass kayaks on first descents down the best western white waters. Always, there were flocks of children participating in every adventure and experiment. I thought the Craigheads might be the only family in America that was having more fun than the Kennedys. Obsessed with falcons as I was from birth, I read *My Side of the Mountain* in 1964. When I met Jean Craighead George that day in New York, she reminded me about the letter that I had written her, at age eleven, politely inquiring if she knew where I could find an occupied kestrel nest. The following year, my father finally bought me a pet-store red-tailed hawk. I manned her to my fist although I still lacked the tutelage to train or hunt her.

But in the autumn of 1968, I entered Millbrook School in upstate New York, drawn by its informal falconry program. At Millbrook, just across the Hudson from Delhi—where Sam and Frightful had had their adventures—I found a small cadre of students who not only shared my devotion to the birds, they had mastered the sport of falconry. That autumn, we captured and trained red-tails and kestrels, immature birds on their first migration. We used bow nets, bal chartris or harness pigeons, and contraptions that bristled with monofilament snares and nooses which we found diagrammed in Beebe & Webster's *North American Falconry and Hunting Hawks* or described in the classic writings of Frederick the Great.

By the time the leaves fell in the third week of October, we had trained the birds to come when we called and to follow like dogs, but high in the canopy flying from tree to tree over our heads. We beat the bush below them for cottontail and pheasant, worked the corn stubble for giant Belgian hare and the forests for red and gray squirrels. We flew falcons and goshawks but mostly wild red-tails, pioneering many of the game-hawking techniques still used by American falconers.

I don't think any of us realized how unusual our success in training red-tailed hawks to hunt was until we all made a pilgrimage to see Al Nye the following Thanksgiving in Falls Church, Virginia. Nye, one of the fathers of modern game hawking, flew peregrines and goshawks, the classic choices of traditional Asian and European falconry. Nye showed us his prized European goshawk, Suzie, and boasted that the bird had already taken a dozen cottontails that season. When we told him we'd taken around the same number with our red-tails, he reacted skeptically. Convention considered the North American red-tail to be at best an inferior hunting tool. European falconers dismissed them contemptuously as "buzzards." We told Nye, "We have the pelts to prove it."

We talked about hawks every spare moment—at meals, between classes, and after chapel. At night, we fashioned hardware, hoods, jesses, and gauntlets and bewits out of tough, pliant kangaroo hide. We marked in our memories the raptor nests we found during our daily winter hunting excursions when no leaves obstructed our view of the upper canopy. In the spring, we climbed up to those nests to band baby red-tails, crows, and owls. We learned to use ropes and climbing spurs to scale the tall oak and ash trees where the large raptors nested. I also learned taxidermy and basic veterinary skills, how to determine disease, check for worms, give injections, and diagnose a range of illnesses and parasites that afflict raptors and other animals. We even began a raptor breeding project, one of the first in history, and were partially successful, persuading a golden eagle and a red-tailed hawk to lay eggs in captivity.

Since my years at Millbrook, I have flown hawks nearly every autumn. These days, I am flying a pair of Harris hawks. I have flown my hen, Cuchin (a superb hunter), for fourteen years. I continue to trap, band, and release hawks every migration on Orange County's Schunnemunk Ridge—a vantage from which, on a clear morning, I can glimpse the Catskill peaks around Delhi. On a good day with a south wind, we trap upwards of fifty hawks: peregrines, Cooper's hawks, sharp-shins, red-tails, goshawks, merlins, and golden eagles. I maintain breeding aviaries for hawks and owls at my home in Mount Kisco, New York, a few miles from Jean George's home. I breed quail, pheasant, and occasionally turkeys, and I operate a wildlife rehabilitation center, with state and federal licenses that allow me to rehabilitate orphaned and injured raptors. My experience as a young falconer accounts in large part for my lifelong devotion to raptors and my continued interest in natural history.

Our time as falconers left its mark on my schoolmates as well. All of them have chosen careers in the natural sciences or as environmental advocates with exceptional records. For each one of them, reading *My Side of the Mountain* was the formative inspiration of their falconry experience. My years as a falconer helped drive my own career choice as an environmental lawyer and advocate. The knowledge and experience I acquired from falconers have marked my life and made me a far more effective advocate on nature's behalf. I have to assume that thousands of other children outside my immediate circle were also inspired to varying degrees of ecological stewardship by their exposure to Sam Gribley's adventures in *My Side of the Mountain*. It's my hope that this wonderful sequel, *Frightful's Mountain*, will inspire thousands of new kids.

ROBERT F. KENNEDY, JR.
July 1999

Frightful's Mountain

Frightful, the peregrine falcon, could not see. A falconer's hood covered her head and eyes. She remained quiet and calm, like all daytime birds in the dark. She could hear, however. She listened to the wind whistling through pine needles. This wind music conjured up images of a strange woods and unknown flowers. The sound was foreign. It was not the soft song of wind humming through the hemlock needles of home.

Frightful was a long way from her familiar forest. Suddenly an all-invading passion filled her. She must go. She must find one mountain among thousands, one hemlock tree among millions, and the one boy who called himself Sam Gribley. The one mountain was her territory; the one tree was Sam's house; the perch beside it, her place. And Sam Gribley was life.

Frightful Takes Off

Frightful had not been quite two weeks old when she first saw Sam Gribley. He had lifted her from her nest on a cliff. Small as she was, she had jabbed him with her already powerful talons as he carried her to the ground. "I'm going to call you Frightful," he had said. "You are a raving beauty." Then he carried her to the gigantic hemlock tree on the mountain and into its hollowed-out bole. This was Sam's home.

He fed her four and five times a day. He carried her on his gloved fist and talked to her. Before long, Frightful thought of him as her mother. He nurtured her like a peregrine falcon mother would.

When she was older, Sam made a perch for her and placed it outside his tree. He taught her to fly to his hand. When she was full-grown, he took her hunting with him. By now, the memory of her parents was pushed far back in her mind. Sam was her family.

At night and on winter days, Sam brought Frightful inside the huge old tree. She perched on his rustic bedstead and warmed herself by the clay fireplace. On spring and summer days, she would sit on her perch outside and watch the birds, the butterflies, and busy Sam. Patiently she waited for him to take her hunting. It was her greatest pleasure. She loved the sky. She loved the updrafts and coiling winds, and she loved "waiting on," hovering above Sam until he kicked up game. Then she stooped, the wind singing in her feathers.

Frightful was an excellent hunter who rarely missed. The food was shared. Their lives depended on each other. She must find Sam again now.

Frightful crouched to fly. She could not see. She folded her gray-blue wings to her body and straightened up.

Hooded and tethered, she had traveled with two strange men for several days.

One of them had taken her from the perch beside the big hemlock tree. He had a deep jerky voice and a face like a condor's. She looked intently at him before he slipped the falconer's hood over her head.

Sam had begged and pleaded with the man not to take her away, but he had pushed Sam aside and carried her down the mountain to a pickup truck. A leather perch had been presented to her feet. She had stepped up on it as Sam had taught her to do. A door had closed, and she was inside a camper on the truck. The motor rumbled, and she was moving. A falcon bell tinkled nearby. A sharp-shinned hawk had shifted his feet. A prairie falcon called out a single note. They, like herself, were sensing the direction of the moving pickup—east, northeast, east, then straight north.

Several feedings later, the second man put Frightful on a perch in the pine forest. The prairie falcon and the sharp-shinned hawk were there, too. She could hear their bells tinkling. Although they were birds who would readily attack her, she was not afraid of them.

Frightful was a peregrine falcon. She was faster and more agile than any other bird or beast the world around. Her long pointed wings; wide shoulders; and strong, tapered body were sculpted by the wind, the open sky, and the nature of her ancestral prey—swift birds.

Frightful sat calmly under her hood, turning the sounds in the pine forest into mental images. A song sparrow caroled. A cardinal chirped. They told her she was in a forest clearing edged with bushes where song sparrows and cardinals lived.

A northern waterthrush trilled. Frightful envisioned a dashing stream shaded by a majestic forest, the summer home of the northern waterthrush. She heard the stream in the distance. It had many voices as it spilled down a stairway of rocks.

Suddenly the cardinal screamed an alarm. A predator was approaching. The songbirds stopped chittering. The forest became silent. Even the insects ceased stridulating. Frightful pulled her feathers to her breast. The enemy was low and coming toward her.

The sharp-shinned hawk flew off his perch in terror. His bell tinkled. He was stopped by his leash, which was knotted to a steel ring at the base of his perch and to the jesses on his legs. He jumped forward, fell back, and beat the earth with his wings.

A killing snarl colored the air red.

An eastern coyote had killed the sharp-shinned hawk. The killer, bird in her mouth, ran toward her pups in the woods. With a jerk, she, too, was stopped by the leash. She turned back and dug at the base of the perch until it toppled and fell. The next sound Frightful heard was the clink of the ring at the end of the leash bouncing over the ground. The sounds faded into the woods.

A wind twisted Frightful's silky pantaloons of pinstriped feathers, which hung down over her enamel-shiny legs. Her tail flicked. She was nervous.

Human footsteps approached.

Their sound did not conjure up the image of the men she had been traveling with. Wary, she lifted her wings to fly.

A hand touched the front of her legs, and she stepped up onto it as Sam had taught her to do.

"Hello, Frightful." Her name; but not Sam's voice. The tone was soft, like the call of a mourning dove.

"What are you doing here?" the voice asked, and Frightful recognized Alice, Sam's sister. In her mind's eye, she saw a rosy face with sea-blue eyes and yellow hair. Frightful relaxed. Alice was family.

She liked Alice, who ran and jumped. She also darted. Frightful liked movement. A spot in her eyes that connected to many nerves gave her an instant focus on movement. Running, leaping Alice was a member of Frightful's home forest. Sam must not be far away. Frightful eased her grip on Alice's bare hand. She lifted her talons.

"Frightful," Alice said softly. "You've got to get out of here." The young girl's voice brought back images of the one mountain among thousands of mountains, the one hemlock tree among millions of trees—and Sam.

"I'm cutting your jesses," she whispered. "You are surrounded by enemies! Fly, fly far away.

"Fly away, Frightful! Sam is not allowed to have you. He has to have a falconer's license, and he's too young to get one. Fly, Frightful! Fly far!"

A quick slash of a knife, and Frightful's jesses and leash dropped away. The hood was flipped off.

And Frightful could see.

"Fly!" Alice urged.

Frightful saw the clearing before her and the leaves on the bushes, even the shiny needles at the tops of the pine trees. Her eyes were endowed with incredible vision.

Alice tossed her into the air.

Pulling on her powerful wings, Frightful sped to the top of the tallest pine and alighted on a slender twig. Her large, black-brown eyes observed the forest, the cascading stream, a town tucked into a steep valley, and rolling mountains as far as she could see.

She turned her head almost all the way around, but could not see or sense the one mountain among thousands of mountains, the one tree among millions of trees. She must get higher. She flew. Strong wing beats carried her into a thermal, a column of warm air that rises from the sun-heated ground in a spiraling bubble. She got aboard and circled upward a thousand feet.

The view was still unfamiliar. To the northeast the rolling mountains ended in a steep escarpment. A waterfall plunged down it, falling two hundred feet to the ground. Beyond the escarpment stretched a valley almost obscured by industrial haze. Rivers threaded through it. Directly northward the rugged Adirondack Mountains stood in a green haze above the land.

Frightful had not been fed for ten hours. She was desperately hungry. Her first act of freedom would be to hunt for herself.

But the forest was not the habitat she knew. Sam had trained her to hunt in abandoned fields. She circled and waited for him.

He did not appear. Frightful flew higher. A movement on the ground caught her eye. Alice was walking on a road that wound through the pine forest. Frightful pumped her wings once and plummeted earthward. When she was twenty feet above Alice's head, she scooped her wings, dropped her secondary feathers, and braked herself. She hovered, "waiting on" for the girl to kick through the fields and scare up the game as Sam would have done.

Alice did not look up. Her eyes were on the road. Presently she came out of the forest into open farmland. Frightful's eyes sought movement. This was the kind of country she and Sam hunted. Tipping one wing, she moved effortlessly over an abandoned field. She waited on for Alice.

But Alice did not come into the field. She stayed on the macadam, where nothing lived. She was in a hurry. Breaking into a run, she dashed around a bend, just as a yellow-white-and-brown dog with long ears and droopy eyes left his hideout in a culvert. He saw Alice run past him. Crouching, he pulled his tail between his legs and dropped out of sight in the daisies. He had been beaten as a pup and was terrified of people. He was thin, but not skinny, for he lived quite well on the mice and rabbits in the field. The farmer who saw him from time to time called him Mole. Every time he lifted his gun to shoot the dog, Mole disappeared in the ground. The man had Mole pegged for the killer of his chickens.

Mole slipped silently through a thistle patch. A pheasant burst up. Frightful rocketed earthward. She struck the bird a mortal blow and dropped with it to the ground. Instinctively she covered the food with her wings to hide it from other predators. She plucked but did not eat. She was waiting for Sam.

Mole smelled the dead pheasant and lifted his head above the thistles. Alice was gone and, seeing no other humans, he followed the scent of the game. Suddenly he burst upon not just a pheasant, but also Frightful. He stopped. Frightful lifted her feathers and threatened him. Then, holding the heavy bird in one foot, she beat her wings and skimmed over the thistles. She gained height and sped away and up.

Like a lightning bolt, a red-tailed hawk swept under her and, upside down, grabbed the pheasant in his talons. Frightful was pulled a short distance before she opened her feet and let go of the food. Four crows flew out of the woods and chased the red-tailed hawk.

Two crows saw Frightful. They turned away from the red-tail and, cawing frantically, dove at her.

Frightful flew into the leafy shelter of a maple tree growing along a fencerow.

"Come harass the falcon," the raucous crows called to each other. The message traveled swiftly, and crows came flocking to the tree. Two dozen gleefully pestered their enemy.

Frightful ducked the black bombers until she could stand them no longer. Taking flight, she sped around the barn and into a pine tree at the edge of a woodlot. She alighted close to the tree trunk, where her dark back feathers and striking black head would blend with the bark. The crows did not see her and returned to their nests.

The excitement of the hunt and chase had tired Frightful. She rubbed her head on her broad shoulder, fluffed her breast feathers, and rested. Her lower lids moved up over her eye and met the upper lids. The image of the one hemlock tree among millions filled her mind's eye and then faded. She was asleep.

Frightful awoke as the morning sun brought color to the tops of the trees. Still ravenously hungry, and growing weak from lack of food, she left the pine and circled above an alfalfa field.

A mouse came out of its den and chewed on a grass seed. Frightful threw up her wings and dropped. She never completed the stoop. The male red-tailed hawk shot out of the woodlot. Wings pumping, he was on a bullet-straight path for Frightful. His mate sped to his left.

Frightful saw the hawks coming, maneuvered her wings, and shot herself up into space like a rocket. High above the red-tails, she looked down. Now she had the advantage. She was above them. To all birds anything overhead is a threat. The hawks beat a fast retreat to the woods. The female lit on a bulky stick nest where four nestlings huddled. Frightful had been in the territory of two devoted parents who were defending their young against a falcon.

Frightful put distance between them by climbing higher. A mere speck in the sky, she took a reading on the polarized light of the sun. The rays vibrated in lines that told her the direction. She sensed the one mountain among thousands, the one tree among millions—and Sam. She must go there.

Mindful of the red-tailed hawks, she flew north to get beyond their territory before heading for the mountain. In moments she was looking down on the escarpment and waterfall. They touched a memory of the right world for a peregrine, a memory as old as her species' time on earth. Drawn to the cliff and the waterfall, she flew lower and lower.

On the top of the escarpment stood Alice. She was under a spruce tree, staring up at it.

Frightful soared toward her.

Two goshawks, the lions of the woodland birds, suddenly dropped out of the trees and dove at Alice. They skimmed over the blond head and climbed skyward. In the top of the spruce tree sat four young goshawks. Alice was discovering, even as Frightful had, the fury of parents protecting their young.

Alice shinnied up the tree trunk, grabbed a limb, and climbed toward the nest tree. The female goshawk rose, dove, and rose again, her huge feet with their black talons poised to grab her flesh. Alice swung an arm and fended her off.

"Alice! Duck!" Sam's voice.

Frightful's world was suddenly right. Sam was here. The two would go hunting. She would catch their breakfast, and he would hold her on his hand and feed her. He would talk and whisper to her.

She waited for his three-note whistle that meant, "Come to me." There was no whistle.

"Come down, Alice," Sam shouted.

"No," Alice shouted back.

The girl climbed on. She broke off the dead limbs, pushed back live ones, and wiggled upward. Near the nest the male goshawk struck Alice's backpack a powerful blow, nearly knocking her out of the tree. Sam leaped to the lowest limb and climbed. The huge female goshawk dove at him. He held out his foot to fend her off. Her talons slashed his moccasin.

Frightful swept down from the sky and perched in an oak tree, waiting for Sam to go hunting.

Alice climbed into the bulky nest. She picked up a baby goshawk and tucked it into her backpack.

"Sam can't have a falcon," she said to the bird. "But you are a hawk. You'll love Sam."

Quickly she scrambled over the edge of the strong, revamped crow's nest and started down the tree. Sam saw her coming and climbed down too. He jumped to the ground. A moment later Alice dropped beside him. The raging goshawks attacked again.

Sam pulled Alice into the shelter of the woods. The goshawks followed screaming, until the two enemies disappeared under a clump of mountain laurel.

Then the goshawks saw Frightful. They attacked her head on. She twisted, confusing them, and climbed swiftly out of their reach.

When Sam and Alice came out of the woods, the winged lions bombed them again. Taking advantage of this, Frightful dropped over the edge of the escarpment. The goshawks did not see her.

She landed on a rock that stuck out from the cliff and shook the excitement out of her feathers. Behind her was a cave. She walked into its shelter, then out. It was comfortable and safe, but she was too weak from hunger to stay there. A day and a half had passed since she had eaten. Stepping to the edge of the rocky overhang, she looked for food.

She saw movement on the cliff. Sam was standing under a jutting overhang not far from her. With one powerful stroke of her wings she was above him.

"Creee, creee, creee, car-reet," she called. This was her name for Sam Gribley.

"Did you hear that?" Sam exclaimed to Alice.

"Frightful," she shouted.

"No other bird but Frightful uses my peregrine name." He stepped to the edge of the ledge and looked up.

"Frightful!" he called.

She scooped her wings back then forward and hung above him.

"Creee, creee, creee, car-reet," she called.

"She's free, Alice," Sam cried. "She's not dead. I was sure she was dead."

No whistle told Frightful to alight on Sam's hand. She waited for this command, sculling her wings. An updraft carried her higher. She looked down. Still Sam did not call her to his hand. And because he had trained her so well, she could not alight without his whistle.

Confused, she let herself ring upward on a thermal, peeling off at a great height. Then she flew out over the valley. She must hunt for her life.

But she could not. Sam was her mother. She needed him. He needed her. She turned back.

This time she hovered before his face.

"Creee, creee, creee, car-reet," she called.

"Hello, yourself, Frightful. Hello, hello."

"Call her down, Sam," Alice screamed. "Whistle for her."

He did not.

Frightful flew higher—waiting.

Another draft of warm air swept up the escarpment, struck her open wings, and ringed her up again. She rode this thermal to the top, where the air was cool and could not lift her any higher.

Closing her wings to her body, she dropped headfirst almost a thousand feet, braked, and waited ten feet above Sam.

Again he did not call her.

A strong wind gusted. Frightful tipped one wing steeply, turned, and glided with the flow out over the valley. Above the Schoharie River turbulent air waves tossed her up, down, and sideways. She closed the slots between her flight feathers and maneuvered the bumps like a mogul skier.

"Cree, cree, cree." One of her own species was calling her. She turned her head and saw a male peregrine falcon. The tiercel caught up with her, then passed beneath her, flying upside down. He was so close she could hear his contour feathers buzz in the wind.

"Chup, chup," he sang. Frightful slowed down, instinctively recognizing the love song of the male peregrine falcon.

"Chup, chup." He flew on his back again. He rolled in loops, then once more on his back. He took her talons in his.

"Chup."

Although the time of peregrine courtship was over, and other males and females were feeding young, this male was seeking a mate. Frightful found herself responding to him. Holding her wings steady, she followed him on a steep descent. Vortices of air spiraled out from her wing tips, sending golden hemlock pollen twisting in circles.

Then she saw Sam at the top of the spruce tree. He was returning the little goshawk to its nest. Frightful turned back.

Chup chased her. He made an awe-inspiring loop and cruised upside down beneath her. Gently he held her talons again, and a new feeling brightened Frightful's mood.

"Chup, chup, chup," the tiercel called as he flew ahead of her. This time Frightful caught up with him. They flew in tandem above the Schoharie Valley.

I N   W H I C H

Frightful Goes to Falcon School

Chup led Frightful higher and higher, to the misty bottom of a fair-weather cumulus cloud. Frightful left him. The fuzziness of clouds, even thin clouds, was distracting to her. She liked clear air.

Soaring back toward the escarpment, she scanned twenty miles in all directions for the one mountain where the one gigantic tree grew. She did not see the mountain.

From out of nowhere bulleted the female goshawk.

Frightful shot up into the protection of Chup's cloud. The goshawk turned back.

"Chup!" The tiercel appeared in the mist, flew close to her, then dove earthward at a steep angle. Again his "chup" touched some deep peregrine memory in her, and she followed the daring tiercel.

Seconds later he thrust out his feet and landed on a cliff ledge. Frightful thrust out her feet and came down not far from him. She was on a stony rampart above the Schoharie River. The cliff and the river spoke to her of her first home and her parents. She held her wings to her body and stacked her tail feathers. She was agitated. The scene was familiar and unfamiliar.

Chup walked toward her, lowering his head in deference to the greater size and power of the female peregrine. "Cree," she responded, and relaxed.

But for size and Frightful's almost black head and cheek straps, Frightful and Chup looked alike. Both had large black-brown eyes, set deeply under flat foreheads. Their beaks were ebony black with saffron-yellow nares. White throats and cheek patches shimmered above pale breast feathers stippled with black flecks. Their wings were long and graceful instruments of speed. They sat erect. They held their heads high. Their beings were lit with an inner flame and, at the same time, the cold stillness of ice. They were the royalty of birds.

Frightful quickly took in her situation. The cliff was about sixty feet high and set back from the river. The land below was bottomland, where red maples, trees of the wetlands, grew. Geese and ducks paddled among cattails and sedges that lined the river's edge. Bank swallows popped in and out of nest holes on the far riverbank. Directly below the aerie was a pine tree where two blue jays had built a stick nest. In it were four scrawny nestlings. Chup let them live. They were part of his aerie community, like the flowers and the huckleberries.

Frightful had arrived in perfect peregrine habitat. She was only vaguely aware of this. Almost her whole life had been spent with Sam on a mountain. Sam and his forest and abandoned meadow were her habitat.

She looked at Chup. He bowed his head to her. His respect awoke Frightful to action. She stretched her neck high. She lifted her feathers to look larger and therefore more beautiful to the tiercel. With this feather talk she told Chup she was bonding with him. She felt a closeness to this pleasant member of her species.

Then a slight movement provoked her to peer behind Chup.

Three young peregrine falcons stared at her. The eyases sat on their bums, legs stretched out in front of them. They were very young, no more than a week old. Their plump bodies were covered with white down; their beaks and feet were gray like the rocks. They were huddled on bare earth in the middle of a garden of pink blazing-star flowers.

"Psee psee," each one cried. "Feed me." The sound stirred a new feeling in Frightful. She leaned down as if to

pluck food, then, not knowing what came next, she stared at Chup.

Chup picked up a half-eaten duck and delicately snipped off a small bite. Folding his talons under his toes, he walked to an eyas and placed the morsel in her open mouth. He pulled off another bite and then another, feeding the chick until she was quiet. When the other two called "psee," he fed them morsel by morsel, patiently, devotedly.

Frightful watched, her own terrible hunger mounting.

When the wobbly eyases stopped eating, Chup broke off a bite of duck and offered it to Frightful. She swallowed ravenously and waited. She was back in her pattern with Sam. When Sam fed her she waited to see if he was going to give her just a bite and take her hunting again, or carry her home to feast and rest. Chup was not part of this routine. He offered no more bites, nor did he take her hunting. Instead he left. He flew off to do as the peregrine tiercel must do—hunt for his mate and young, until the chicks were well feathered and could keep themselves warm without being brooded. When that happened, the female mate would join in the hunt.

Not Frightful. She looked at the duck Chup had left. According to Sam's training, it was hers. Gingerly at first, then ravenously, she fed herself. Death by starvation comes quickly to a bird of prey, and strength returns as quickly. With each bite her eyes began to glisten with energy, and, like a flame, she soon flickered and stood tall.

Vitality restored, she lifted one wing and stretched it as far as it would reach. Then she stretched the other, wiped her beak, and sat contentedly.

Two days ago Chup's first mate, mother of the chicks, had flown out to stretch and exercise after days of inactivity. She had not come back. When several hours had passed and the chicks were screaming, Chup knew she had been killed. That afternoon he searched for another mate. The eyases must live. He called the love song over cliff and river. No female appeared.

That night he brooded the eyases. He fed them in the morning. He hunted at noon when the air was slightly warmer and he could leave them unattended. As he hunted, he looked for a mate.

High above the escarpment he saw Frightful hovering above Sam Gribley. He called her, but she paid him no heed. When, however, she rode a rising thermal and passed near, he rolled and danced for her. He flew upside down for her, touched her feet. When she began to notice him, he lured her toward his motherless young, but she was not easily won. Once more she turned and flew away. On the third attempt he succeeded.

With Frightful at the aerie, Chup's world was right again. His chicks had a mother.

But all was not perfect.

Frightful, who for most of her life had been raised by Sam—not by peregrine falcons—had much to learn.

She did not know what to do with three eyases that looked like wobbly birds, not like Sam. When Chup left, she stared at them curiously. They stared back. The smallest one, a tiercel, shivered. His chilled wings beat the earth like a drummer's stick. Frightful tilted her head, the better to see Drum's movements. They were telling her something.

"Psee," he cried in peregrine baby talk. The sound reached down into Frightful's early memories of her mother. She drooped her wings. Drum cried again. Instinctively she turned under her piercingly sharp talons, and stepped over the shivering eyas. He trembled. She raised her feathers and sat down. Drum wiggled into her warmth. Feeling his little body against her brought her into the brooding mode of the birds. When the other two nestlings crept into her feathers, she went into a trance. A goshawk flew overhead; a rock fell off the cliff and bounced past the blazing-star flowers. Frightful did not move.

"Psee," Drum called. After he had been brooded and warmed for an hour, he was suddenly voraciously hungry. He looked up at Frightful and screamed for food. With a start she came out of her trance, stood up, and shook her feathers.

"Pseeee, pseeee." Drum screamed louder. His open beak was bright red and rimmed with yellow. It was a bull's-eye that guided a parent to the mouth. Frightful saw the target and was inspired to tear off a small bite of duck. She held it in her beak, not knowing what to do next. Drum was too young to reach up and take it, and she did not lean down to put it into his mouth. She held the food in her beak above him. He did not take it, and after a short time she swallowed it.

"Psee, psee, psee." Now all the chicks were calling. They pressed up against her, their red and yellow mouths wide open, their wings fluttering. Frightful was overwhelmed by demands she did not understand. The one hemlock tree among millions came to mind, and she lifted her wings to fly.

Chup appeared in the distance. She recognized him a mile and a half away, although a mere speck. He grew larger and larger until he landed, full size, with a soft rustle beside her. In his feet was another duck. He presented it to Frightful and waited for her to do what came next—take it to a plucking perch away from the aerie, defeather it, then feed it to the eyases; the loudest, most aggressive first.

But Frightful did not carry it to a plucking perch or pluck it. In her past, Sam had prepared the food.

She did sense from Chup's stare that she should do something. So she preened her flight feathers, wiped her cheek on her shoulder, and walked under an overhanging rock. She hid from the screaming chicks. Chup waited patiently for her to do her part. She put her head in her shoulder feathers and closed her eyes. The eyases screamed. Chup could wait no longer. He carried the bird to his own plucking roost and prepared it.

"Psee, psee, pseee," the chicks screamed as he returned with the food and dropped it at Frightful's feet. He must hunt. She must do the feeding.

Frightful did not. She looked at the duck and then away. The eyases cried relentlessly, their eyes wide, their necks trembling from hunger.

That message reached Chup. He leaned down and snipped off a tender morsel. Lady, the largest of the two female chicks, bolted to him, stepping on Drum in her rush. She opened her mouth, and Chup fed her bite after bite. Then her sister, Duchess, pushed her aside and begged for food. Chup fed Duchess, too.

When the little females were satisfied, Drum reached up to Chup. At that moment a movement in the valley caught Chup's attention, and, good provider that he was, he left the aerie to catch a pigeon. Feeding was not on his agenda anymore.

Frightful saw Chup capture the bird in midair. She was interested, but when another pigeon flew by, she did not go after it. Sam had trained her to hunt the rabbits and pheasants that lived in the abandoned fields on their mountain. She turned her back and ate duck.

Drum screamed and screamed.

Frightful knew she should do something. She held food for the tiercel again. Drum opened his mouth and reached up. Brooding the fuzzy, white eyas had calmed him down once. She opened her feathers to him and sat down. He nestled up against her and stopped screaming.

Frightful felt his warmth against her body like a messenger of love. Ill-equipped as she was to be a mother, she called softly, "Cree." *I love you.*

Hours later she got to her feet and walked to the duck. Drum hobbled behind her. When she stopped and leaned over the food, he wedged himself under her. She tore off a morsel. Her head was low and he snatched the bite from her. She did not mind. Frightful plucked another bite for herself. Drum took that bite and the next until he was satisfied. Then she ate.

For the next week Chup fed Lady and Duchess and

hunted for the whole family. Drum had learned to get food from his strange mother.

The eyases grew their second, heavier coat of natal down when they were about fourteen days old. With that development they could regulate their temperatures. That was the signal for Frightful to go hunting. She did not. She kept brooding the chicks and letting Drum take food from her. Chup fed Duchess and Lady.

Despite their unorthodox lifestyle, all five peregrines prospered.

The chicks grew rapidly. As their flight feathers appeared, their white down disappeared. By the time they were four weeks old, they were almost full-grown and testing their wings. They needed food, lots of it, and Chup could not fulfill their demands. The eyases screamed and yelled constantly. It was time for Frightful to hunt.

On a late June day when the cliff side was green and yellow with chickweed, Chup caught a passing starling on the wing. Frightful was excited by his victory and flew out to get the bird. Chup winged above her and dropped it. She turned upside down and caught it in her talons.

The feat awoke a deep instinct in Frightful. She carried the bird back to the aerie and plucked it. But she did not feed the chicks, nor did she eat it. Not being hungry herself, she left it at the scrape and flew to a rock ledge above the aerie.

Drum ran to the bird. He tore it open and ate. His sisters ate. Despite their new mother, the timetable of peregrine development was taking care of them. The young peregrines were old enough to feed themselves—and to attack their parents.

Frightful moved out of the aerie to a pine stub. Left alone, the eyases explored the flowers, the rocks, and the crevasses in the cliff. Lady picked up a feather in her beak. Duchess took it from her. Lady rocked back on her rump and threw up her feet. Duchess threw up her feet. They locked talons and pulled. Drum jumped on a moving feather and tossed it into the air. As it spiraled downward, he rolled to his back and snagged it in his talons. Frightful watched them curiously. They were playing peregrine falcon games she had never learned. High on her stub, the young fed, Frightful pulled one foot up into her feathers and sat quietly.

From a distance Chup saw that Frightful was not going to hunt. He flew back and called her. His voice was insistent. Frightful flew to him.

Chup led her out over the valley, saw a duck, and plunged. Frightful sensed she should hunt ducks, but could not. Chup was gone. She rode a strong wind eastward, her wings outstretched, her feet pressed against her tail, the sun shining through her feathers.

She was over the escarpment and waterfall. Recalling the goshawks, she changed her direction. As she flew over the woods, she saw the young goshawks with their parents. They were chasing crows and adroitly maneuvering among the tree branches. Their broad, short wings were designed to speed them in and around trees and branches. Frightful was a bird of the open sky. She climbed high above them.

The landscape passed swiftly under her, and in mere moments she was above the pine forest where she had been a captive of the two strange men and where Alice had set her free. Frightful searched the macadam road for the girl and was over the abandoned field.

Mole slid out of the culvert and sniffed his way along a small mammal trail. Frightful flew above him and waited on. This dog, like Sam, scared up game.

Mole wove through the grasses. A rabbit leaped up, and within seconds Frightful was on the ground, game in her talons. But Mole was there, too. The falcon and the dog looked at each other. Mole dropped down on his belly and snarled. Frightful covered the food with her wings.

Mole lunged for Frightful. In a flash, game in her talons, Frightful and the rabbit were in the air. She flew several hundred feet before coming down. Mole, keeping low and out of sight of the farmer's gun, sneaked up on her. Again he lunged. Frightful took off, hit a strong updraft, and was lifted over the field and barn.

She heard Mole barking irritably as his food went flying away.

She did not see the farmer come out of his house with a shotgun, nor did she see Mole dash into the culvert. Frightful was over the goshawk nest, and she was flying hard.

Frightful set her wings and glided above the waterfall and cliff to the Schoharie Valley. She descended gracefully to her aerie with food for the eyases.

IN WHICH

The Eyases Get on Wing

Drum, Duchess, and Lady glanced at the rabbit. It was not part of their food vocabulary, so they kept right on screaming. They were hungry for waterfowl or land birds.

Frightful ate the rabbit while the eyases watched, twisting their heads from side to side and calling "pseee" when she swallowed. Duchess walked up to her, screaming in earsplitting decibels. Then the eyas lifted her wings and attacked. Frightful backed off a few steps and stared at the young falcon. Lady and Drum lowered their bodies horizontally and charged Frightful. The eyases had become dangerous. They were practicing for the competitive world they would soon face. Frightful wanted no part of this schooling. She lifted herself into the air, fanned her wings, and flew to her tree stub.

Chup came home. He brought no food to the eyases. Duchess charged him, mouth open, feathers lifted. He sat still and panted in the sun. His feathers were rumpled and he held his head low. Chup had not eaten for a day and a half. He was weak. That did not matter to Duchess. She attacked him. Chup, like Frightful, was forced to leave.

Alighting on the dead limb of an oak, he looked down and saw the rabbit. Without hesitating, he dropped down onto it and ate, fending off the eyases. He could still dominate them.

Chup had catholic tastes. He was nine years old. Each winter he migrated to South America. When the El Niño rains changed the balance of nature and birds were scarce, he dined on mammals and iguanas. Rabbit was food, and he was hungry.

Lady and Duchess stopped screaming. Chup was eating rabbit; it must be food. Painfully hungry, Lady led a raid.

She sneaked up to Chup. When he covered the food with his wings and body, Duchess reached in from the rear and snatched the rabbit. She tore off small bites but did not like the taste. She shook her head and sent the meat flying against the rocks. Chup finished eating and flew off.

Drum, who had now seen both parents eat this new food, dragged what was left under the overhang. Taking a bite in his beak, he swallowed. It was not delicious, but it was satisfying. He plucked another bite, then another. Drum was a survivor.

When he was satisfied, Duchess and Lady tried the strange food again. They ate gingerly, partially satisfying their hunger.

By sundown the peregrine family was fed if not full, but more importantly the family had a new housing arrangement. The eyases were now old enough to attack anything in sight, including their parents, and with that, their parents had sensibly turned the aerie over to them. Frightful and Chup did not return to the nest site. Frightful slept on the stub of the pine tree, Chup on the dead limb of his oak.

That evening they all watched orange and pink clouds float against a turquoise-blue sky. Chup felt restless. His offspring could not only eat on their own but also defend themselves. Just before sundown he spread his wings and soared out over the valley. He climbed high, he spiraled down, he skimmed along the river. With quick wing pumps he shot up and out of sight of Frightful and the eyases. Just before the sun set, he sped earthward, landing lightly on his dead branch. He heard the eyases chittering, saw Frightful sitting erect on her stub, and let his nictitating membranes slip across each eye. His lower eyelids closed upward and cut out the last of the daylight. The cliff side was quiet. The peregrine family was on schedule with summer. The eyases were completely feathered, feeding themselves, and aggressive, and the parents were perched alone.

With the help of Mole, Frightful now regularly brought food to the eyases. Each morning she flew southward to Mole's farm and brought back strange but nourishing foods, which she dropped to the youngsters. Chup, who had gotten thin doing the job of two parents, began to put on weight.

Mole also gained weight. The old hound had the canniness of a wolf. It didn't take him long to realize he had a hunting companion who was quicker on the pickup than he. The first two times Frightful went off with the game he had flushed, he could do nothing but bark. Then he learned that she didn't like groundhogs. She had tried one and abandoned it to him. She also didn't like skunks or rats. He chased them all. She got the rabbits and pheasants. He got the rest.

Mole and Frightful went hunting almost every day. When they had harvested the most conspicuous and abundant animals of the farm fields, Mole led her to more distant fields. The animals they left behind would breed, and their offspring would breed, until there were too many for their food supply. Then the two hunters would return and adjust the numbers again.

When the fields yielded little game, they worked the barnyards and farm gardens. Together they kept the rabbits and groundhogs from eating the farmers' crops and the rats from eating the corn stored in cribs and bins.

And so Frightful hunted with Mole, as she had hunted with Sam, and became the provider Chup and the eyases needed.

The eyases grew properly. At five weeks of age they were as big as their parents. Only a few bits of down on their heads and shoulders and their brown-gray color told how old they were.

On a hot day in early July, Duchess sat at the edge of the aerie, her wings lifted to keep her cool. A wind blew over her. It moved more rapidly over the top of her wings than under them and created lift. Up she went. She hung above the ledge for a moment, became confused, and stalled herself out by moving her wings and changing the wind flow. She fell back to the aerie.

Lady faced the wind, lifted her wings, and was airborne. She, too, fell back. She sat on her heels. Something new and wonderful had happened to her. She had been in the air with space between herself and the cliff. She and the wind had managed this wonder, which had changed her sense of who she was. She was a bird. She must fly.

A few minutes later, Duchess flapped her wings. She was lifted up and over Lady's head like a bit of thistledown. She alighted on a rock, where, somewhat astonished, she looked down on Drum and her sister. From them she looked into immeasurable distances—above, below, and to all sides—then nervously preened her feathers.

Frightful came home with a rabbit and dropped it in the aerie. Duchess jumped to get it, fell, spread her wings, and sailed. Quickly closing them to her body, she dropped down on the aerie. She ate what was now delicious rabbit to her.

That afternoon a thunderstorm darkened the river valley. Chup came home from his hunt. Retreating to his dead limb, he watched the lightning buzz around the cliff. Frightful flew from her stub and walked under an overhang near the aerie just as rain poured out of the clouds. The eyases crouched against each other, holding their feathers at slight angles that shed the water in rivulets. They shook, cleared water from their eyes with their nictitating membranes, and listened to the thunder boom.

When the storm passed and the sun came out, Chup set out over the valley, not to hunt, not to check on populations of doves and ducks, but simply to fly. He coasted on downwinds, rode like a water skier on turbulent winds, and soared on light breezes.

Frightful followed his flight with her keen eyes until he disappeared in a cloud. Then she left the rain shelter and returned to her tree stub. She sat quietly.

From the aerie, Drum, Duchess, and Lady watched everything that moved. The ocular pectin in their eyes had developed. They could see the movements of an ant walking as far away as the distant river. They studied and noted and memorized. They collected visual memories that would serve them for the rest of their lives.

Drum, fascinated with his acute vision, walked to the edge of the aerie to watch young swallows in their nests in cliff holes across the river. A wind struck him from the side; he flapped his wings to keep his balance and he, too, was flying. He soared along the cliff and landed with a crash on a ledge about a hundred feet away. Elegantly he folded his wings to his body and stood tall. He watched the rainwater fall from the leaves of the forest below and a tree frog vibrate his throat with song.

Suddenly Frightful plummeted out of the sky and landed beside him. Drum called, "Pseeee," and opened his beak to be fed.

Chup, who was soaring under the purple-blue cloud bottoms, saw Frightful with the fledgling and flew down to his dead limb. He called her away from Drum. The fledgling must survive on his own. Once again Frightful's early training did not help her with peregrine protocol. She heard Chup scolding her, but remained with Drum. Companionship with Sam had colored her concept of life. Young, old, bird, boy, girl, dog—companionship was comforting.

Early the next morning she flew off to hunt with Mole. Drum awoke and stared at the valley. Crows winged past, calling out messages to family members to stick together. A leaf spiraled toward him on an updraft. He did not try to fly again. Mother would come back.

Frightful did return to Drum with a rabbit late in the morning. Drum did not eat it. He had not cast a pellet this morning. Birds of prey eat meat, bones, feathers, and fur. They absorb the nourishment and cast out the indigestible parts in a tidy pellet. They cannot eat again until the pellet is cast. Drum sat quietly, food before him, waiting for his body to go through this cycle.

Duchess and Lady saw Frightful bring food to Drum and set up such a screaming demand that Frightful picked up the rabbit and carried it above the aerie. She dropped it to them. Chup watched her.

Frightful saw the food fall onto the blazing-star leaves and seedpods, then flew to a tall hemlock at the top of the cliff. Sitting among the lacy needles, the image of the one mountain among thousands, the one tree among millions, and Sam came to mind. She scanned the horizon for her home, then forgot it. Duchess now had her attention.

The young falcon was running to the rabbit with out-stretched wings. The air flowed over them and under them, and before she could stop herself, she was off the ground and in the air. She flapped and sailed out over the red maples. High above them she stalled out and fell, landing in a treetop, her wings spread across leaves and twigs. She hung there for a moment, her shiny legs dangling. One foot found a sturdy limb, and then the other. Awkwardly folding her wings to her body, Duchess stood upright on the tree limb and shook out her rumpled feathers. When she was comfortable, she looked around. Food, companions, and parents were out of reach. She must fly to survive.

Meanwhile, Lady went over to the rabbit and stuffed herself. She napped in the noontime heat, opening her beak to pant and perspire. Upon awakening she played with a feather, then a stick. Feeling restless, she stretched her wings. The air picked her up, and Lady was flying, too. She flapped to the pine tree where the blue jays had nested, landed, and lost her balance. Thrashing her wings, she righted herself on a limb. Spellbound, she began to stare at the silver river. It moved.

Out of reeds and willow trees sped a flock of red-winged blackbirds. They flew up and circled around her. Tiny, fearless birds, they screamed and dove. They skimmed by

her head. They struck her with their wings. Duchess ducked and dodged and finally decided to leave. Flapping her wings uncertainly, she jumped off the limb and headed for the aerie. The blackbirds cried louder and dove at her like pellets of hail. Not far from the cliff face, Duchess lost her lift and fell down through leaves and twigs. She came to rest on a royal fern. It bent under her weight and lowered her into the fern bed. The red-winged blackbirds could not see her and flew back to the reeds along the river. Duchess sat in peace, but also in fear. How would she get airborne again, buried down in the windless and wet fern bed?

Drum, who had finally cast his pellet, eyed the rabbit in the aerie and set off to walk the short distance for a meal. He flapped his wings to help himself over a bramble bush and was flying. He hit a thermal and went up. Holding his wings firmly outstretched, he spiraled high above the cliff. The air was cold at the top of the thermal, and the warm bubble vanished. Drum fell earthward. He hit the ground, spreading his wings and tail to cushion his fall.

Drum got to his feet and ran to a bush. From the bush he flew to a cedar tree, and from the cedar tree to an oak at the edge of the cliff-top woods. He flew, hopped, climbed to its crown, and looked down on the vast valley the river had carved. He saw Frightful on her stub and let out a wild call for food.

Chup answered from above. He dove, scattered a flock of ducks, and brought one back to the aerie. He dropped it without slowing down, then flew over the cliff, over Frightful, over Drum, over the woods, and out of sight.

IN WHICH
The Wilderness Tests the Eyases

Frightful watched Chup wing over her pine stub at the edge of the cliff. She had no desire to follow him.

Her attention was riveted on the fledglings. Duchess

was in a red maple, Lady was out of sight in the fern bed, and Drum was perched in an oak tree behind her. Not one could reach the food she and Chup had dropped in the aerie—unless they flew.

No peregrine instincts told Frightful how to get the fledglings on wing. She sat and waited until it became too dark to see.

Lady awoke hungry. She was cold and wet. She shivered as she shook the water from her body and wings. Flapping hard, she struggled to fly out of the fern bed.

Duchess, on the other hand, did not seem to care if she ever flew again. She was comfortable. A dove flew past her. She focused on it with keen interest. A robin sang. She stared at it, then settled dreamily on her limb.

Drum had another agenda. Seeing his mother on the pine stub, he called pitifully, "Pseeeee pseee." She did not look at him. Desperately hungry, he jumped toward her, spread his wings, and was sailing like a paper airplane toward the ground. He hit the grass and stopped, *kakak*-ing in fear. Frightful heard him but did not answer. An ancient peregrine instinct was finally guiding her—do not feed the fledglings.

Drum hunkered down where he was for most of the day. As evening approached, he lifted his feathers to keep warm. A damp, cold wind rolled along the ground and over him. Drum hopped into a huckleberry patch at the edge of the cliff and lay down on his stomach.

Frightful closed her eyes. The flatness of the stub under her feet reminded her of her home perch. She could see her mountain, the hemlock, and Sam. Her mothering was coming to an end.

At dawn the next day she looked about. She preened, then touched the gland near the top of her tail and lubricated her dry feathers with its oils. She glistened.

A heartfelt "pseee" from the cliff top reached her ears. Drum thrashed out of the brambles into view. He saw Frightful and cried again. She stared and sat still.

Drum's "psee" became an angry "kak, kak" that tripped him into action. He beat his wings and took off. He dropped—down, down, down. He alighted on the aerie, scattering the seeds of the blazing-star flowers with the blast of air from his wings. With a hop and two flaps, he was upon the rabbit.

Duchess saw Drum eating. She spread her wings, soared out of the red maple, and landed with a thud close to him. He lifted his feathers to scare her, but she was bigger, and bigness is boss in the peregrine's world. Duchess grabbed his food. Then she saw the duck. She preferred bird to mammal and jumped on the duck. Running, covering, walking, she took it behind the blazing-star garden and ate ravenously.

Lady, who was at the foot of the cliff, was cold and losing weight rapidly.

"Psee," Lady called over and over. Neither father nor mother came to her rescue. She fluffed her feathers to warm her body and sat still to conserve energy.

When Drum had eaten his fill, he walked toward Duchess. She lifted her wings and chased him to the edge of the aerie. She screamed, "Kak, kak, kak," and he took off. He soared over the trees, tilted one wing, and found himself headed for the cliff. He pulled up on his tail, down on his wings, and was climbing. He came over the top of the cliff and steered to his oak tree. Drum was flying.

Duchess, alone and full of food, sat in the clumps of blazing-star flowers and stared down on the blue-green landscape. Her sharp eyes widened. Far away she saw a gray fox. He was walking along a tree that had fallen across a meandering stream. The slender animal stopped at a limb, then walked down it and jumped to the ground. He disappeared in the fern garden.

Duchess looked away from the fox. He was too big to be food. She walked to the edge of the aerie. Suddenly she spread her wings, was lifted by an updraft of wind, and spiraled skyward on a warm thermal. As she balanced herself with wings, feet, and tail, she felt the new and wonderful sensation of flight.

The thermal collapsed, and Duchess fell landward, alighting on the limb of an enormous sycamore tree near the river. Birds were all around her—on the water, in the reeds, in the trees and sky. She stared at the different kinds. Each species moved differently. Ducks ran on the surface of the water to get airborne. Pigeons banked and turned en masse in the sky. Swallows dipped and darted. Rails kept low in the marshy river edges. Cranes flew laboriously, then swiftly.

She chased the birds but could not catch any of them. After many hours, she flew home to the aerie and food.

Following Lady's scent, the gray fox located her exact position with his nose and leaped. She was gone. He looked up. The young falcon was climbing the cliff, beating her wings, taking hold of rock cracks with the hook of her beak and her talons. She scrambled and flopped. The fox climbed after her.

Frightful suddenly appeared above him. She dropped headfirst, pumping her wings close to her body, and hit the fox with her talons. She was going twenty miles an hour. He yelped and leaped. Too heavy for Frightful to hold; she let go.

The fox fell, lit on his feet, and ran into the woods.

Frightful returned to her stub.

Lady struggled on up the cliff. With a last effort, she pulled herself over the aerie ledge and flopped down on her breast, wings out. She rested with her beak on the ground. She was exhausted.

"Psee," she cried weakly, unable to reach the remains

of the rabbit. Frightful saw her struggle, but she did not help. Lady was out of the nest. She must make it on her own.

Hours passed. The young falcon grew more feeble. She was near death.

Chup sped into view. He dipped above Lady and dropped a pigeon. At the sight of the food falling her way, Lady felt a powerful desire to live. She flipped to her back and snagged the pigeon before it hit the ground. She rolled to her belly and tore off small bites. Energy rushed through her body, and she lived.

Three young peregrines had survived their first flights.

By the end of August the juvenile peregrines were catching almost all of their food. They wandered farther and farther from the aerie.

On a sunny day Lady flew far down the river valley. She lit on the tower of a church in a small town. Along the street were elegant Victorian homes. An elderly man emerged from one, walked to the churchyard, and scattered birdseed. Down from the trees, window ledges, and rooftops flocked many pigeons. They dropped to the man's feet and ate.

Lady did not go back to the aerie. In the days that followed she grew strong and fat.

Drum stayed near the river. He was a stunning juvenile

tiercel. He had his mother's dark head and his father's pale, blue-tipped body feathers. Like his father, he hunted the traditional food of his species—ducks and other waterfowl.

One evening, flocks of terns came to the river marshes. They were down from Alaska and Canada, migrating ahead of a cold front. In the few days they lingered in the Schoharie Valley, Drum grew fat on them. Then one dawn the birds took off for the south, and Drum went with them. His food was migrating; he must follow. In less than two days he and the terns and willets reached Delaware Bay.

When the September winds blew the downy milkweed seeds to new soil, Chup was gone, too.

A week later Duchess sensed another cold front bearing down from the northwest. She took a reading on the sun's rays and, pointing her beak south, she, too, departed. With her went little cedar waxwings and juncos.

Lady sensed the high pressure of the same front and she, like Drum and Duchess, began the long pilgrimage of the peregrine falcon to warmer climates.

Frightful was alone, the only peregrine falcon in the Catskills who had not migrated. She was thin. She had not put on the extra layer of fat birds need before instinct tells them they are ready to go. She lingered at the aerie, hunting the nearby fields. At night she returned to her stub.

Without the fledglings to feed she grew heavier, but weight alone was not enough to start her migrating. There were three signals she must feel: the fitness of her body, the rightness of the environment, and the chill of the atmosphere. She felt none of these.

Three weeks later, when orange, yellow, and purple leaves were showering down from the trees, Frightful was fat. Food was now scarce, and snow was in the air. She faced south. All the signals said go. But she did not.

Time passed; snow flurries came and went. Thousands of birds flew south. She watched them, lifted her wings to migrate with them, then folded them back in place. She could not go.

Early one morning a cold wind sent shivers through Frightful. She got aboard a thermal and ringed up. On it was a lone red-shouldered hawk. At the top of the bubble the hawk snapped its wings and shot south. Frightful hung there. She was looking down, not southward, searching for the one mountain, the one tree, and Sam. They were not to be seen. She got off the thermal and dropped back to her stub.

She dallied another two weeks. The window of the fall migration is open for only a few months. Once closed, the messages from body and environment shut off, and it is too late to go.

For Frightful that would be disaster. There would not be enough food for her to survive in the frigid northern winter.

I N W H I C H

Frightful Peregrinates

When a light snow covered the Schoharie River Valley, Frightful's bird sense urged her one last time to leave or die. She took a reading on the sun's rays, listened to her internal compass, and started south.

She covered only ten miles before she turned back. She was hungry. She would find Mole.

When she was over the pine woods where she had been held captive, she flew faster. Mole's farm was ahead. Speeding swiftly, she overshot the farm. It had changed. The weedy fields where the game lived had been leveled and their black soil turned over in neat rows. The dense bushes along the fences, where many birds lived, had been clipped. She circled the culvert. It, too, was changed. The bushes that covered its entrance were gone. The culvert was a round, bare hole.

"Creee, creee, creee," she called.

Mole did not come out.

Frightful circled the farm again but did not find the yellow hound. She flew to the silo. The air was bumpy where warm currents met cold. She rode the waves to the ledge of the silo and stepped under the jutting roof. The veins of her flight feathers were split and dry. She oiled them, then snapped them back in line by running her beak down the shafts from base to tip. She let go with a flick that triggered the veins to fall neatly into place. This done, she was sleek and ready to hunt.

Frightful surveyed the landscape. Even the woods were different. The leaves had fallen, and the red-tailed hawk nest was empty. The parents and young had migrated to warmer lands.

Weak from hunger, she left the silo and flew back over the culvert. She waited on for Mole. The wind tossed her. She matched each burst with a twist to stay in place, but Mole did not come out.

Behind her, purple-red and blue-gray clouds forecast rain and wind. It was urgent that she find food. Swooping along fencerows to scare up game, she searched intently. Nothing stirred.

Twilight sent her back to the silo ledge, her hunger raging.

Hours later she was awakened by thunder shaking the old silo. The dark night was lit by flashes of lightning. With each flash she saw dancing trees and wild water pouring across the barnyard. It gushed out of Mole's culvert. The flashes became almost continuous, then stopped. The rain pummeled, swished, pattered, and was over. She went back to sleep.

At sunrise the sky was white-yellow and pale blue, the colors of a rain-cleansed day. The woods and farm sparkled with freshness. Frightful flew over the culvert and waited on. Mole did not make an appearance.

She was growing weaker. Spotting a distant harvested cornfield, she flew to a tree at its edge. She waited for something to move. Finally she caught a mouse. The storm had driven the bigger game into their shelters and burrows. In the late afternoon Frightful flew back to the culvert.

Out of the sky plunged a bald eagle. He aimed right at her. She back-flipped, and he missed. The eagle beat his wings and got above her for another strike. He dove. She rolled to her back, threw up her feet, and raked him with her sharp talons. He flew up to strike again. Frightful dropped to the ground and, as the eagle dove once more, ran into Mole's culvert. He lost sight of her. He climbed, circled the culvert once, then boarded an air current that carried him off toward the Hudson River. He would spend the winter fishing there.

Safe inside the culvert, Frightful panted from fright, then quickly became calm. Bird emotions are intense but short. She glanced at her surroundings. The gushing storm water of last night had slowed to a trickle. She drank. Refreshed, she walked to the mouth of the culvert, saw no eagle, and sprang onto her wings. She climbed high and fast over the tilled field.

When she was high enough to feel safe, she leveled off. An undulating wind rocked her southward over a brushy meadow. She came down on a fence post and watched for food. She was growing feeble as hunger weakened her.

Suddenly she was in deep trouble. The sun was setting. In mere minutes the light would be too low for her to find a roost. She flew up into the last light. It illuminated the bell tower of the abandoned church at Beaver Corners. She headed for it.

Winging to its weathered and rotting peak, she landed gracefully. The churchyard was thick with weeds. A farm and a woods lay nearby. She had been here. She shifted her weight nervously as the condor face of the man who had taken her from Sam flashed into her visual memory. She felt fear, but it was too late in the day to move on. She forgot him.

Snow patches lay under trees where the sun did not fall. A migrating Cooper's hawk dropped into the nearby woods for the night. Like Frightful he, too, was late.

The sun set. The sky turned a twilight purple. Frightful could see only light and dark shapes. She flew down to the sill of one of the four glassless windows in the church bell tower. Lifting her wings, she walked into a square, moldy room and jumped up onto a rusted bell lying on its side. Every window was black with night. She shook her feathers and, weak from hunger, fell into a restless sleep.

Last night's thunderstorm had preceded a cold front. The temperature dropped below freezing, and the migration of the birds stopped. The robins and wood thrushes and other small birds that navigated by the stars at night fluttered down into the trees. They sought the warmth of the wind-breaking woods to wait for the cold front to pass.

At dawn they tittered among the trees. They called to each other and ate insects numbed by the cold.

It was also too cold for hunger-weakened Frightful to fly on her way. She must eat.

She took off from the tower and flew out over a weedy meadow. A rabbit jumped up and ran toward a thicket of spiny hawthorn trees. Hunger sharpened her skills, and Frightful was upon it before it reached the fortress.

No migrating eagle passed overhead; no barred owl saw her. She ate, her strength returning quickly. The leftovers she carried back to the bell tower.

The cold did not let up for days. Frightful and the thrushes stayed on at Beaver Corners.

In the middle of one night the warmth returned. Wings rustled like taffeta as the birds lifted themselves out of the woods and continued their migration. Frightful opened her eyes. Ribbons of birds were flying across the yellow face of the moon. The birds were navigating by the shining light of stars.

In the morning the haze of an Indian-summer day erased trees, fields, and roads. Frightful could not see well enough to fly. She shifted her feet restlessly. The one mountain among thousands, the one tree among millions, and Sam were coming more vividly to mind the longer she lingered.

On an unusually warm day in early November, she stepped to the open sill of the bell tower. She had caught no food for two days. She must move south.

Frightful tried to read the angle of the sun's rays, but a gray-blue haze cut them out, and she could not get their message. She turned her head from right to left. She felt tiny iron particles in her brain lining up with the earth's magnetic field. She needed both the sun's rays and the magnetic field to plot her course. She had only one.

She took off anyway.

Frightful headed southwest.

She flew over the town of Berne and the steeples of North Blenheim. She chased a night heron up the Schoharie River, lost him, pursued a mallard duck, and lost her. She was not trained for birds. She stopped chasing them and came down to rest on a spruce tree on the banks of the Schoharie Reservoir.

The air was dense with moisture; clouds thickened and darkened the sky. Around noon they let go. Rain poured down. Tree trunks became rivers and spruce needles waterfalls. Frightful was her own tent. Water ran off her head and shoulders, her beak, and her tail. No wetness seeped through her feathers. When the rain blurred her eyes, she cleared them by flashing her nictitating membranes like windshield wipers. She sat calmly in the deluge.

A lost great blue heron took shelter on a limb below her. Frightful looked at it only because it moved. The bird was too big for her to take.

A wind hit the forest in strong gusts in the afternoon. Clouds circled clockwise. The edge of the last tropical storm of the year had twisted up from the south and was drenching the Schoharie Valley and Reservoir.

Rain fell for two nights and three days. Frightful

dropped lower on the spruce tree and waterproofed her feathers with the oil from her tail gland.

The deluge slowed, the clouds circled counterclockwise, and a flock of spotted sandpipers blew in from the coast. They ran the shore edges like windup toys and snatched minute bits of food. Frightful turned her head away. Her natural prey, the waterbirds, still did not interest her. Sam's training had faded somewhat under Chup's menu, but game from the upland meadows was still very much her idea of food.

The sun came out. Frightful flew to the top of the tallest spruce. Although the day was windy, all the guideposts she needed to orient herself were readable. She found the longitude of the Atlantic flyway, the migrating route of the birds of the east, and the magnetic field of the earth. She flew. She was going away from the one mountain among thousands, the one tree among millions, and Sam. She was going south to warm weather and food.

Catching an air current that took her up and over a mountain, she looked down on acres of open fields, meadows, and grassy clearings. Here lived the food she liked. She coasted down to the roof of a small cabin. It was Woodchuck Lodge, the mountain home of nature writer John Burroughs. Before Frightful could gather her wits, a chipmunk, abroad on the nice day, snatched some grass seeds and ran under a mammoth boulder and was gone.

Around the rock were drifts of snow, now sodden from the tropical storm. A plaque marked John Burroughs's grave.

Frightful brought herself to attention. She must eat. Concentrating, she looked at every twisting grass blade and bobbing seed head. Suddenly she drew in her feathers and stretched her neck. The mountain laurel by the lodge was shaking. Frightful lowered her body to strike.

Out from under the porch came Mole. His ears and coat were plastered with autumn's burrs and Spanish needles. Around his neck was a collar. Mole had been on an adventure.

The adventure had taken him far from the culvert.

While Frightful was watching the young peregrines learn to hunt, Mole's run-down farm had been sold. The new owners were aunt and uncle to Hanni and Hendrik Van Sandtford, friends of Sam and Alice Gribley. Hanni and Hendrik had come over to Altamont to help their relatives restore the neglected farm. They had cleared brush, tilled the abandoned fields, and leveled the overgrown fencerows.

Their work done, they were driving home in Hendrik's pickup when they saw a dog slinking along the side of the road. He wore no collar to say he was a pet. Hendrik stopped the truck, and Hanni jumped out. Mole vanished into a culvert. After many kind words and tasty food offerings, Mole finally trusted Hanni enough to creep into the cab. He cringed at her feet all the way back to the Van Sandtford farm.

At the farm, Hendrik combed the burrs from Mole's hair and gave him a bath. Mole was embarrassed. He put his tail between his legs and hung his head. Next Hendrik put a collar around his neck, snapped a leash to it, and dragged him, protesting, all the way to the barn. A bed of sweet straw, water, and ample food were put down. Mole dug under the straw and hid. He refused to eat. Hendrik sat with him late into the night, talking softly.

Mole heard "good dog" many times and then his new name, General. He listened to the kindness in Hendrik's voice and finally ate and fell asleep as the sun was coming up.

Two nights later he chewed through his leash and jogged west. He crossed the bridge at Gilboa and climbed into the forested mountains.

He hunted, slept, and came out of the trees at Woodchuck Lodge. The layout looked good to Mole. Weeds, briers, and the grasses told him there would be rabbits, pheasants, woodchucks, and mice. He sniffed around the lodge, found no scents to say the house was occupied by people, and squeezed under the porch. Near the chimney base he clawed out a cozy wolf bed and settled in.

Although Mole was happy to be away from people and bedded down in his own home, he was faced with a problem. The cold had sent the woodchucks into their burrows for the winter. After a few days of fruitless searching, he trotted across the field, headed for the town dump he had passed on his way up the mountain.

"Creee, creee, creee."

Mole stopped. Sniffing the air, he looked up. Frightful was sitting on top of the lodge, feathers shining in the autumnal light. He stared at her.

She cocked her head and stared at Mole. She did not wonder at finding him again, just opened her wings and flew out over the field. Mole broke into a run and, nose to the ground, worked the grasses and dead goldenrod spikes. A rabbit burst up. Swift as light, Frightful was upon it. She pumped her wings and carried it away without coming down to the ground. When she was almost to the lodge, a great horned owl saw rabbit and falcon, sped silently out of the woods, and sank her talons into the food. Thrown off balance, Frightful fanned her flight feathers, regained her equilibrium, and went after the owl. Owl and rabbit vanished into the woods. Frightful, a falcon of the open skies, did not follow. She pushed down on her wings and up with her tail and came to rest on the porch railing of Woodchuck Lodge. Mole was right behind her.

The two looked at each other, then the old hound turned and went back to his hunting field. On the second try they caught a pheasant. This time Frightful scanned the sky for thieves before flying with it to the rooftop. Daintily she ate choice pieces.

Mole sat on his haunches, looking up at her, his tongue hanging out, his mouth drooling. He wanted his share of that food. Suddenly he growl-barked so viciously that he scared Frightful. She took off, leaving the food behind. The bird rolled down the shingles and fell to the ground. Mole picked it up and, tail wagging, carried it under the lodge. There he feasted.

Frightful had eaten enough to bring back her strength. She flew to a tall tree and perched. The bright sun was warming the fields and meadows, creating a twisting and invisible bubble. On it rode a lonely peregrine tiercel. He circled up and up. Frightful opened her wings. Lift took her into the thermal. She spiraled to its ceiling. The tiercel peeled off and shot south like a missile.

Frightful was next. She circled the top of the bubble, tipped her wing, and spread her tail. Everything was right—the angle of the sun's rays, the wind, the temperature, and the magnetic field of the earth. She ripped through the sky like a meteor.

Her wings spread in glorious flight, she looked down on the vast landscape.

And there it was. The one mountain among thousands of mountains, the one tree among millions of trees, and somewhere there, the one boy.

Frightful turned abruptly west and in minutes was over the mountain. Snow lay on its highest levels. Food would be scarce here.

She flew back to Woodchuck Lodge. There the last weak messages from the environment pointed her southward again.

But she had seen the mountain.

Confused, she *kakak*-ed in distress and flew into the spruce tree for the night.

I N   W H I C H

Frightful Finds the Enemy

The next day was cold. Sleet and rain fell on the Catskill Mountains. The air currents dropped steeply earthward, making it difficult for Frightful to fly. She flew above the trees but could not get high enough to see her mountain again.

Chilled and tired, she came back down to the spruce tree near the lodge to wait for the ice storm to pass.

Mole holed up under the house. The sleet had driven the game birds and animals into retirement, and he knew it was useless to hunt. However, unlike Frightful, Mole had another option. Around noon he trotted off to the town dump. At dusk he returned refreshed.

For the next few mornings Frightful watched Mole leave the lodge and return in the evening. His tracks were soon covered by snow and icy rain, erasing all signs of the hound's travels.

One evening Mole did not return from the dump. Frightful spent several days hunting without him. She caught a mouse running over the snow and a squirrel that had ventured from its leaf nest.

When Mole finally came back, he was limping. His left ear was torn and bleeding. He had lost a fight for a female Labrador on a farm down the mountain. He squeezed under the porch and did not make an appearance for several more days. When he did emerge, he eagerly hunted the Burroughs fields, and Frightful joined him.

The sleet, snow, and cold kept Frightful confined to the mountaintop at Woodchuck Lodge. Finally the air currents stopped dragging her down, and she flew high enough to locate her mountain, but the entire western horizon was swathed in clouds. She went back to the spruce tree.

At last a high-pressure bubble brought sunshine to the icy Catskills.

Frightful shook out her feathers and preened and oiled them. She lifted her head. Her large, round eyes searched for the indicators that would guide her on her way. She found none. The window of migration had closed for Frightful. She was a winter bird, one who cannot go south.

Like all winter birds, Frightful's life was threatened.

But the day was clear. The sun sparkled on the ice and snow, and the wind blew the last clouds away. Frightful left the spruce tree and climbed up and up. When she reached two thousand feet high, she saw at last the one mountain in thousands. She flew straight for it.

Gliding over densely wooded White Man Mountain, her eyes pinned on Sam's mountain, her position fixed, she heard a familiar cry.

"Cree, creeee, creee."

She dove down and skimmed the tops of the trees. Duchess was somewhere below.

"Cree, creeee, creee." The call directed Frightful's eyes to a perch on the ground. On it sat Duchess.

"Cree, cree, cree," Frightful answered from a leafless maple.

Duchess wore a falconer's hood. She was jessed and leashed. Her juvenile feathers were rich brown in color. She was fat. Duchess was living well.

"Kak, kak, kak." Two goshawks sat on perches not far from Duchess. Beyond the birds was a small hunting cabin set back in a grove of young hemlocks. Near it stood a pigeon cote and a duck house.

The cabin door opened and a man stepped out.

"I thought I heard a wild peregrine," he said, lifting his binoculars. He wore camouflage pants and a sheepskin vest filled with pockets. Around his neck hung a falconer's whistle. Frightful knew the man. One eye was brown and the other eye was blue. He had a condor face. This was the man who had taken her from her perch beside Sam's hemlock tree. This was Bate.

"Spud," he called. "Come here." The door opened, and Spud came out. He was portly and wore a dirty ski jacket.

"What's up, Bate?" he asked.

"We just got real lucky," said Bate. "There sits twenty-five thousand dollars." He pointed to Frightful. "Twenty-five and twenty-five makes fifty thousand. Let's get her."

"Come on, Bate," Spud said. "We ain't got time. Skri's waiting for us. Let's sell these birds before the bird cop finds us and we go back to jail."

"Leon Longbridge is never gonna find us here," said Bate.

"Could," said Spud, peering around. "I saw that falcon guy from Roxbury driving along the lumber road down below."

"Who's he?"

"The guy who came to the sheriff's office and took the prairie falcon and the sharp-shinned to the falconer in New Paltz. He was lookin' hard up-mountain."

"That don't mean nothin'," said Bate. "You can't see this place when you're ten feet from it."

"Well, let's get out of here anyway. He knows we were in jail for selling falcons and hawks to wealthy Saudi Arabian falconers. That's a federal offense. Remember?"

"They let us off light."

"Yeah," said Spud, running a thick hand through thinning hair, "but a second offense is federal prison, and that's a long stay. Let's go."

"We can catch this bird in minutes," Bate said. "Her crop is empty. She's hungry. Probably lost on migration.

"Twenty-five thousand is a lot of dough." He focused his binoculars on Frightful again.

"Go get the mist net," he said. "I'll get a duck for our pretty duck hawk. That'll get her in the net in two seconds."

Spud hesitated.

"Get goin' if you want to get out of here so bad," Bate said.

Spud hurried into the cabin for the net. Bate walked quietly to the duck house.

"Creee, creee, creee," Frightful called again. This time Duchess recognized her voice. She turned her hooded head almost upside down, then sideways as she listened.

"Pseee, pseee," Duchess answered in baby talk. "Pseee, Pseee," she repeated. Frightful sat quietly. What little instinct she once had had for feeding the young was entirely gone. The nesting season was over. But the baby call brought a feeling of comfort to Frightful. She was a winter bird and a lonely one. She listened quietly.

Bate and Spud, moving like midnight bats, left the cabin and darted through the trees.

Frightful watched them. She closed her wings to her body and pulled her tail feathers together one upon the other. She did not fly.

"Pseee, pseee." Duchess again called the hungry nestling cry, reminding Frightful that she herself was very, very hungry.

She looked for movement. Her eyes went to the men. They were the only action. She watched them stretch a long mist net between trees. It rippled, then went taut and almost disappeared from sight.

Bate took out a duck from his vest pocket and, holding her in his arm, stroked her breast until she was hypnotized and calm. Then he tethered the Muscovy on the other side of the net from Frightful.

"All set," he whispered to Spud. "Follow me." He led him in a wide arc away from Frightful and back to the cabin.

"She's still there," Spud said as he opened the door. "I'll stoke up the woodstove while we wait. It's chilly."

"Don't bother," said Bate. "As soon as the Muscovy flaps, that falcon will dive and hit the net."

"I hope so. I don't like this."

The Muscovy came out of her trance and shook. Frightful saw her. She tensed to dive.

Bate watched through his binoculars.

"There she goes! We got her," he said.

"Not yet," said Spud. "Let her get real tangled in the net. We've waited this long; a few more minutes won't matter."

Frightful straightened up. Ducks were not prey. She was still Sam's falcon. Waterfowl did not interest her.

"Cree, creeee, cree," Duchess cried. The Muscovy heard the falcon cry and flapped in terror.

Calmly turning her back, Frightful took a bearing on the sun's position and beat her strong wings. She flew straight for the one mountain among thousands, the one tree among millions, and Sam.

IN WHICH

Disaster Leads to Survival

The wind carried Frightful speeding down the side of White Man Mountain. As she came over a logging road, a man walked out of the leafless November woods. He was dressed in a tan jacket and pants and strode with a gait as free as Sam's.

"Creee, creee, creee, car-reet." Frightful called Sam's name.

With a swift wing beat she alighted above a transformer on an electric utility pole. The man was not Sam. She lifted her wings to fly.

A wind gust knocked her off balance. She tipped, spread her flight feathers like fingers, and braced herself against two wires. Sparks sizzled and burst upward. A powerful electric current shot through Frightful. Her feathers burned. She could not move. The electricity held her prisoner.

She passed out.

Jon Wood saw Frightful get zapped. He grabbed a fallen branch, climbed a boulder under the utility pole, and tried to knock her off the wires. He brushed her, but could not dislodge her. Taking the long branch in both hands, he swept it back and forth. Frightful's left wing was pushed from the wire. The circuit was broken. She fell to the ground.

Jon Wood picked her up and folded her wings to her body. He looked at her burned flight feathers. He saw her cloudy eyes.

"A fabulous and rare peregrine," he mumbled, "and she's dead." He stroked her still-warm breast.

"Another utility-pole disaster," he said to himself. Then went on, "I get so angry about this. It doesn't have to happen."

Smoothing Frightful's seared feathers, he opened a large pocket in his jacket and placed her in it. He would report her death to the U.S. Fish and Wildlife Service in Albany. They kept records of the endangered peregrine falcons. The birds, once down to zero in the East, were gradually making a comeback, thanks largely to a falconer, Heinz Meng. He had bred the first peregrines in captivity and, using an ancient technique called hacking, had been able to free them to the wild. Other falconers learned from him, and the peregrine began to recover.

Jon thought of Heinz as he stood on the mountain road. First it was DDT and other pesticides that killed the great peregrines, he mused. Now it's death on utility poles.

His warm brown eyes narrowed.

"This does it!" he said to himself. "All the utility companies have to do is lower one wire so the birds can't touch those two parallel hot lines and complete a circuit. One little adjustment—that's all—and thousands of these great birds would live."

He opened his pocket and peered down at Frightful, thinking, I've written the utility-company manager so many times, my fingers hurt. Today I'm calling the company president.

He strode on down the mountain to the road where he had left his car. Saddened and angry, he drove home, parked near his barn, and walked to a large bird mews.

"Hello, Sammy," he said to a magnificent bald eagle. Sammy was recovering from an accident with an automobile.

"Kak, kak, ka, kleeeek," the bird replied. Jon smiled and looked from the handsome eagle to his own home. He was proud of it. As a young man he had built it himself on acres of field and forest deep in the Catskill Mountains. The house was dug into the hillside to conserve heat. It was shingled with handmade shakes. Jon had trained a falcon to hunt with him. He had planted his own vegetables. When his land was flourishing, he went back home and married a young woman named Susan. He took her to his mountain with some apprehension. "Do you like it?" he had asked. "I want to live here all my life," she answered.

As Jon worked the land and flew his falcon, he saw how important the raptors were to the environment. Some kept the excess birds under control; some kept the rabbits from destroying his garden; others cleaned up the rats, mice, and voles. He studied and became a master falconer with a license from the U.S. Fish and Wildlife Service. He taught his raptors to fly free and come back to the lure, and the next thing he knew, he and Susan were visiting schools with their birds to tell the children of the importance of the birds of prey.

Jon Wood paused before opening the door to his house. He looked out over the silent white mountains and braced himself to tell Susan the bad news.

"Susan," he said as he walked into the kitchen, where she was feeding an owl. "Another zapped peregrine." He reached into his pocket. "Hey!"

Frightful was moving. Astonished, he lifted her up and rested her on the palm of his hand. She looked at him out of bright eyes. Jon grinned in disbelief.

"Susan," he said. "She's not dead. I can't believe it. She was zapped, burned, fried on a utility pole."

"Oh, Jon," said Susan, coming closer. "She looks awful. We should take her to the vet."

"Let's wait," he said. "She looks amazingly perky. We'll jess her and I'll check her out."

Susan opened a cabinet and took out a pair of leather straps. They were jesses. Falconers for three millennia in Asia and Europe had put the exact same kind of straps on the legs of their falcons, hawks, and eagles. The jesses were held in the fingers or clipped to a leash to keep the birds from departing.

Jon stroked Frightful's wings and breast, then held her feet in his hand and her body along his forearm. Taking first one leg between his fingers, then the other, he gave her jesses, then pulled on a falconer's glove. Gripping the jesses, he flipped her upright on his hand.

For a moment Frightful looked around. Finally she roused, shook her feathers, and sat quietly. She was in a house. Gone were the mountains, the woods, and the Schoharie Valley. Unperturbed, she then stared at Jon Wood. He smiled and lifted her close to his face.

"How do you feel?" he asked by making soft peregrine calls.

"Creee," Frightful said, expressing her comfort.

"A peregrine," Jon said to Susan. "A fierce and noble

falcon right out of the wilds of White Man Mountain, and look at her—sweet as a baby."

"She didn't even bate," said Susan. "I've never seen a wild bird that didn't try to fly, get stopped by the jesses, and hang upside down. She flipped up on your glove like a trained bird."

Jon twisted his fist to examine Frightful's breast, then her back and wings. He touched her seared feathers and feet.

"She looks okay," he said, smiling. "I can't believe it. No flesh burns, no broken bones from her fall—nothing. A few blackened feathers. She should be fried black."

Susan moved toward Frightful with the gentleness of a mother bird.

"Hello, lovely lady," she said. "I'm so glad you're all right."

Frightful sensed in Susan the same love that emanated from Sam, Alice, and this man who held her. She roused to express her contentment, then shook. Several burned feather tips fell to the floor. She observed her surroundings. A prairie falcon called softly from another room. A snowy owl clapped his beak and hissed. She saw rooms, tables, stoves, and daylight coming through windows. This was not Sam's hemlock-tree home, but it did not frighten her either.

Jon brushed away a loose feather from her head and put his hand on her breast. Her felt her crop, the upper portion of the gullet where the food first lodges after swallowing. It was empty.

"You're awful thin," he said. "It's late for you to be up north here."

Susan stroked the quiet bird.

"What are you going to do with her?" she asked.

"We'll fatten her up and let her go."

"But not until spring."

"Not until spring," he assured her. "She wouldn't make it." He held Frightful close to his face and chirped at her.

"What are we going to do with her tomorrow?" he asked. "We'll be gone for five days. We have appointments to show our birds at seven elementary schools."

"Maybe Anthony would drive down from Altamont and feed her," Jon suggested. "You know he's an apprentice falconer."

"I have a better idea," Susan said. "We'll take her with us. We'll show the kids what utility poles do to birds."

"Yes," Jon agreed wholeheartedly. "They should see her."

Susan looked in Frightful's dark eyes. Frightful looked into Susan's eyes and on beyond.

"You're mysterious," she whispered. "The migration is over, and yet you're here. You're a wild bird, and yet you're tame. Where did you come from? What do you know?"

Susan tilted her head to delve the mystery, could not,

and turned back to the job of packing canvas carriers with food, hoods, and jesses for the eagle, hawks, owls, and falcons.

"By the way, Jon," Susan said, checking the list one last time, "what were you doing up on White Man Mountain in the first place?"

"Oh, my gosh, I nearly forgot." He dashed to the phone and dialed the number of the conservation officer for the Roxbury area.

"Hello, Peter. This is Jon Wood. Yesterday I saw smoke rising about where Jebb Harper's hunting cabin is. He hasn't used it since he got rheumatism, and he never lends it out. I went up to check it today."

"Trouble?"

"Yes," he answered. "I didn't go too close because I heard a peregrine falcon call near the ground—then men talking. I was unarmed."

"Hmm, what do you think?" Peter Westerly asked.

"Well," Jon answered, "that man Bate and his friend are out of jail, you know. Last spring they were selling falcons to an Arabian agent, and I haven't heard yet that they've reformed."

"True," Peter Westerly said. "I'd better get Leon Longbridge from the Delhi area and go up there. He's been worried about those two ever since he learned that the Arabian agent, Skri, was back in the area. Sounds like they're up to it again. You heard a peregrine falcon, huh?"

"And a goshawk."

"Oh, boy. Here we go."

Jon hung up and told Susan that the falcon poachers were at work again.

"Are you going to help catch them?" Susan asked.

"I wish I could," he answered. "But we have a long day tomorrow and all the rest of the week. Leon and Peter are the ones to do the job anyway."

When Frightful had eaten until her crop was round and full, Jon showed her a perch. She jumped to it, shook her feathers, and settled down. Jon scratched his head.

"She sure is cooperative," he said.

Frightful sensed she was among people who shared Sam's spirit. She turned her head and tucked her beak behind her shoulder.

On her way up the stairs to bed, Susan stopped and contemplated Frightful.

"You know, Jon," she said, "I have the funniest feeling that our guest is a trained falcon."

"I've been thinking that, too," he said. "She's so relaxed. But where did she come from? I'm the only falconer who can have a peregrine in this part of the state."

"What about Roger Hartzbeen?"

"He's still an apprentice falconer," Jon said. "He won't be able to have one for five years."

"Maybe she got away from someone in Canada," Susan offered.

"But she's not name-tagged. Falconers tag their birds in case they get lost and someone finds them."

"She's a very beautiful bird," said Susan, admiring her dark head and large eyes. She came back down the steps and leaned over Frightful.

"I wish you could talk," she said. "I think you have a destiny to fulfill.

"That's it," she said softly. "I believe I've just spoken your name. You are Destiny."

The next day Jon Wood carried Frightful to a large mews on the hilltop and unsnapped her leash, holding onto her jesses. He opened the door.

"Stay here for a little while," he said. "When we all come back from our school trip, this will be your home. It's big enough for you to get some exercise and catch your own food." He turned his fist until Frightful faced him.

"When the birds return in spring, and food is plentiful, I'll let you go. You can fly home." He peered into the calm eyes. "Wherever that is."

Jon talked to Frightful just as he talked to all his birds of prey. They felt his affection for them in his voice and responded to it with lifted feathers and soft sounds. As Frightful listened, Sam came to mind. She called, "Creee."

Jon held her against a padded board that stretched from one side of the mews to the other. She jumped up onto it and looked about. Three sides of the big mews were wooden. A high ledgelike shelf was built into one corner. It somewhat resembled a peregrine's favorite nesting site—a cliff. Frightful did not fly to it. She stayed on the board.

A ceiling protected the mews from rain and snow, but more importantly from the wild hawks and owls for whom anything that moves is fair game.

Sunlight streamed through steel chicken wire on the fourth side. Frightful did not try to fly through it. Jon observed that.

"Susan's right," he said to Frightful. "You have done all this before. Every other new bird I put in here flies into the wire before it learns it's not free."

Frightful shook her feathers, stretched one wing, and glanced out at the mountains. She was facing home and Sam. She pointed her beak in his direction.

Jon went from one mews to another, hooding each occupant and carrying it to his tour van. He picked up a big, fluffy snowy owl and put his nose into the sweet, dense feathers on his head.

"You're going to have fun, Mr. Freeze," he said. "Kids will hug you to death. And that's what you like best of all."

Presently Susan arrived.

"Hello, Destiny," she said, and added, "Creee, creee, creee."

Frightful heard her own language, lifted the feathers on her head, and drew herself up tall. Susan smiled, stepped

into the mews, and took Frightful on her gloved hand. She carried her to the rear of the van and put her in a carrying case. Frightful did not resist.

"Destiny," she said. "You didn't even struggle. You are a wonder." Carefully she latched the holding case, then peeked in at her.

"You are going to change many lives. That's your destiny."

Taking off her falconer's glove, she picked up Mr. Freeze and climbed into the front passenger seat. Mr. Freeze, who had been hatched in an incubator and had never known any mother other than Susan, cuddled in her lap.

The van, with its beautiful cargo, drove off.

At the bottom of the hill, Jon stopped. A state highway maintenance truck was parked across from his drive. Two men were unloading equipment on the side of the road.

Jon stuck his head out the window. "What's up?"

"Bridge repair," shouted a wiry man in an orange helmet. He crossed the road to the van.

"Bridge repair?" Jon asked. "There are no bridges around here."

"Yeah, there's a little one back toward Roxbury. You probably never noticed it. It's just a flat span over a seepage area."

"The potholes need more repairs than that thing does," Jon said.

"Yeah, but we've got orders to repair every bridge in the state, big and little. Governor's decree. No exceptions. New policy since those people died when the hundred-year flood collapsed the Schoharie Bridge. Big political issue—safety."

"When do you start?"

"In a few days," he said. "After that we go on to Margaretville, and then the iron bridge at Delhi. That'll be the first week in May."

"What's the matter with the Delhi Bridge? It's practically new."

"One of the pilings is crumbling from water erosion. But really it's the same thing—governor's decree."

"Well, I guess it's a good idea," said Jon. "But this equipment is an eyesore. I hope you finish in a hurry." The man shrugged and crossed the road to help his fellow workers.

Susan looked at Jon's scowling face.

"It is a good idea, Jon," she said. "The Schoharie Bridge was falling apart for years and years, and no one did anything about it until it killed five people."

"I know. I just hate to have to look at all that industrial equipment at the end of my beautiful road. This is my Eden."

"Creee, creeee, creee."

Jon thrust his head out of the window and looked up.

"Another peregrine falcon!" he said. "What's going on?"

"Creeee." Frightful answered Duchess from inside her box.

IN   WHICH

Hunger Is Frightful's Teacher

The first visit was a middle school in Roxbury, not far from the Woods's home. Jon and Susan arrived quite early. Jon brought the van to the shipping entrance and carried the hooded falcons and hawks into the auditorium. He put the owls in hollowed-out tree stumps on the stage. Round-eyed, they peered silently out of round holes. When all the birds of prey were in place, Susan let some of the students hug Mr. Freeze. The owl chuttered in pleasure, and the kids oohed.

Then the learning show began. Jon held up Sammy, the bald eagle. He spread his seven-foot wings. The kids gasped. Sammy was breathtaking.

Jon named all the birds and flew the prairie falcon from one end of the auditorium to the other. Holding her high, he talked about the important role of birds of prey in nature.

Finally Susan took Frightful out of her carrying case.

"This is Destiny," she said. "She is a peregrine falcon, or a duck hawk, as these wonderful birds were once called.

"She was late in migrating south this year and came over White Man Mountain on a chilly day. She alighted on a utility pole that held a transformer. She lost her balance, spread her wings, and completed the circuit between two wires. She was shocked with electricity.

"She couldn't move. The electricity froze her to the wires."

Susan went on to say that Jon had flipped her off the wires with a branch and carried her home in his pocket, thinking her dead.

"Suddenly," she said to her wide-eyed audience, "Destiny moved in Jon's pocket. She was alive. We could not believe it. The jolt had not killed her, just burned her wing tips. Jon took her in his hands, smoothed her feathers, and jessed her. Then, with all the grace of the peregrine falcon, she flipped herself up on his fist and looked at us."

Susan held her high. "She is a survivor and she is alive. She wears burns that tell about the dangers of utility poles for our wild birds." The children stared at Frightful, and some said they could smell the acrid scent of her scorched feathers clear at the back of the auditorium.

Jon then told the story of how one of his falcons was electrocuted on the wires of the transformer in his field.

"Ahhh," murmured the kids.

"Once a month I write to the utility company and ask them to lower one wire—that's all—just lower one wire one foot. That would do it. Then the birds couldn't touch the two wires and complete the circuit. Thousands of eagles, hawks, and beautiful owls like these could be saved.

"Not getting any reply," he went on, "I telephoned the management. I got the old runaround. 'Push one to speak to Miss Jones; push two for billing; push three to talk to customer service'—and on and on."

A small girl with dark hair and blue eyes raised her hand and stood up.

"Mr. Wood," she asked, "can we write to the utilities president and ask him to fix the poles?"

"Me, too," said the boy next to her. "I write good letters."

There was a clamor of voices. A teacher put up her hand.

"Do you have a name and the address we could write?" she asked. "This would make a wonderful project for us."

"Creee, creee, creee," Frightful called.

"Destiny wants us to write," piped another little girl, and took out her notebook and pencil.

"Creee, creee, creee."

Jon picked up a sheet of poster paper and wrote:

> *Mr. Lon Herbert, President*
> *New York Electric Company*
> *Albany, New York 10579*

He propped the poster against Frightful's perch.
The students bent over their notebooks.

> *Dear Mr. Lon Herbert,*
> *How would you like it if you were walking a wire, slipped, touched another wire, and was zapped—fried so your mother wouldn't even recognize you?*
> *Well, the birds don't like it either.*
> *Here is a drawing of how to change the wires on a transformer so eagles, owls, hawks, vultures, even blue jays don't get zapped.*
> *Sincerely,*
> *James*

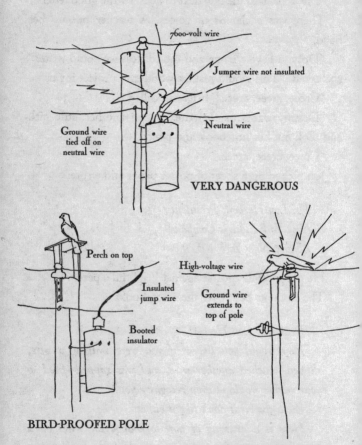

7600-volt wire

Jumper wire not insulated

Ground wire
tied off on
neutral wire

Neutral wire

VERY DANGEROUS

Perch on top

Insulated
jump wire

Booted
insulator

BIRD-PROOFED POLE

High-voltage wire

Ground wire
extends to
top of pole

VERY DANGEROUS

Dear Mr. Lon Herbert,

Birds have rights, too. People cut down the trees and put up electric poles that zap them. I think they should be able to sue you. A bull hit my dad and he sued the farmer and my dad wasn't even dead.

I am going to be a bird-defense lawyer when I grow up.
Andrew.

Dear Mr. Lon Herbert,

We are studying civil rights. The falcons and owls and eagles have no civil rights because you discriminate against them.

Sincerely,
Maria

Jon and Susan carried the letter idea to all the schools they visited, and when the week was over, six hundred were in the mail.

"You know, Susan," Jon said when they were driving home, "those letters just might help."

"Of course they will," Susan replied.

As they came to their drive, they glanced at the bridge-repair equipment, looked the other way, then drove up the long dirt road to their house.

By late afternoon the Woods had returned all the birds to their perches and mews. Jon carried Frightful to hers. He tossed her off his fist and smiled at her.

"Good girl, Destiny," he said. "You just might have saved a lot of birds." He paused. "I hope so." He closed the mews door and walked to the pigeon cote to refresh the pigeons' water.

"Creee, creeee, creee."

Duchess swooped over the cote and climbed up into the sky.

"Creee, creee, creee," Frightful answered.

Jon looked up.

"It's another peregrine falcon," he said. "What is up with you birds? Peregrines in November. Something's out of order."

Duchess circled overhead, then dove over the pigeon cote, sending the birds into panic.

"You're hungry," Jon said as Duchess climbed for another swoop at the pigeons. He was about to release one for her, but changed his mind. He and Susan raised these pigeons for their hawks and falcons to chase and perfect their skills. They were smart pigeons. They always got away. They knew how to dodge their pursuers with twists and turns and disappear in the woods. They would fly around the countryside for a day or two, then return to the cote. Falcons and pigeons both enjoyed the game.

Jon got a rat instead of a pigeon.

He walked into the field, calling to Duchess in peregrine talk. She appeared overhead, prepared to take another swipe at the cote. He tossed the rat. It ran only a short distance before Duchess struck and carried it to a tall spruce behind the barn. She ate for the first time since Bate had turned her loose. He had unsnapped her jesses when he saw Leon Longbridge and Peter Westerly approaching the hideout.

Jon released another rat in Frightful's mews. She watched it dash to the chicken wire and squeeze out.

"Hey," he said. "Don't you know what a rat is?"

"Well, Miss Destiny, the rat crop of New York practically supports our wild raptors now that we've wiped out most of their natural food. And a good thing, or we'd be overrun with rats." He peered up the statuesque figure sitting quietly on the padded board. "And that's a big help to humankind.

"So, I'm going to teach you about rats. You'll need to know all about them when you're on your own." He went back for another. Frightful let it escape, too. It wasn't a rabbit or a pheasant. It wasn't even a waterfowl. She turned her back on the next one.

"I guess you're not hungry enough to learn," Jon said, and gave the friendly call note of the peregrine.

At sunset a fine snow fell. It covered the mountains and roads, the fields and the mews on Jon's mountainside. The owls watched it seep into their homes. The daytime birds slept.

At dawn the Catskill Mountains were white and silent. Frightful opened her eyes on a changed landscape.

The snow fell for two days and nights, and Jon did not feed Frightful all this time. He did come to speak to her and check her burned feathers. The breeding season was over, and she was molting. New feathers were replacing the burned ones.

Susan came to Frightful's mews one day.

"I know you're hungry, Destiny," she said. "But you're being trained. And hunger is your teacher."

She pulled on her falconer's glove and stepped inside the mews.

"Rats are good," she said. "Taste this." Frightful flew to her hand and gulped a large bite of rat. She looked at Susan and called for more.

"I can't give you more," she said, placing her on the padded board. "You learn by being hungry." Susan returned to the house.

The bite of food perked up Frightful. The red-tailed hawk in the next mews moved, and Frightful flew at her, hit the wire, and dropped to the ground. A movement on the sumac bush outside caught her eye, and she flew at a blue jay. The wire stopped her.

That evening Jon opened the mews door and stepped in. He released a rat. Frightful struck it before it had run a foot. She carried it to the padded board. There she deftly used the nick in her beak to cut the spinal cord. It died without pain.

And Frightful ate rat.

Two more weeks of school visits, and several hundred more letters were sent to Mr. Lon Herbert.

Susan called her friend at the local radio station.

"These kids have written incredible letters," she said. "You ought to read them on the air."

The friend was also a bird lover. The following Saturday he asked several of the kids to come to the studio to read their letters. A New York TV station liked the story and sent a cameraman to Jon's house to film the children with Frightful.

The next day three linemen arrived at Jon's door.

"We're here to change the wires on your transformer," said the heavier of the three men, smiling pleasantly. "Also to insulate exposed wires."

"That's just wonderful," said Jon. "But how about changing them all over the state? Changing one isn't going to do much good."

"Three," said the pole climber. "We've been told to change three. Which ones do you want changed?"

"That one on our hill," Jon said, pointing to the pole that had killed his falcon.

"And the one by the Roxbury Elementary School," Susan said. "In fact, it would make a lot of children happy if you fixed all the utility poles."

"Three," said the large man. "Our orders are to fix three."

IN WHICH

Frightful Finds Sam

In early March the first of the migrating falcons and hawks returned to the Catskill Mountains. Frightful was in her nuptial plumage. She had molted completely. The scarred and broken feathers were gone. The white on her tail and under her chin was as bright as new snow. Her back was thunderhead blue, her rose-tinted breast had the brightness of cloud tops. Her head was almost black. She was healthy, and educated in rats and pigeons.

She knew the pigeons and their flight patterns especially well. Her mews faced the cote, and she watched the birds long hours. She saw how they dodged Jon's young falcons with twists and turns. She saw them return home to the cote on smooth, slow glides.

Jon noted Frightful's interest in the pigeons and rats, and on a bright but chilly morning he carried her to the top of his mountain. Susan hurried behind him, jumping patches of soggy snow.

Frightful cocked her head as Jon took off her jesses. She stood free but did not fly. Drawing herself up tall, she mapped the direction to the one mountain among thousands, the one tree among millions. No spring force pulled her north with the returning falcons. She was home, and not far from Sam.

Jon touched her beak with his finger. Susan hugged her arms to her body and watched wistfully. She loved and hated the moment when they set birds free.

"Good-bye," Jon said, and cast her from his hand with a

strong thrust of his arm. Frightful bulleted into the sky and opened her wings.

Susan called, "I'll miss you, Destiny." She moved closer to Jon.

"Oh, why do I get so involved with these birds?" she asked. "It's so hard to tell them good-bye."

Jon nodded and concentrated on the disappearing speck.

"I wonder why she's going toward Delhi?" he finally said. "That's the last place in the world for a peregrine falcon to nest. No cliffs over there."

Frightful knew exactly where she was going. She sped into the wind and covered the thirty miles to the one mountain among thousands in less than ten minutes.

She dropped down onto the one hemlock among millions and came to rest.

"Creee, creee, creee, car-reet," she called.

There was silence, then, "Frightful!"

Sam put down the plumping-mill crossbar he was repairing and jumped to the rock by Baron Weasel's home. Frightful peered at him through lacy hemlock limbs.

"Frightful!"

She dropped down three limbs.

"Frightful." Sam's voice lowered to a whisper. "You came back."

She hopped down to the next limb and looked for her perch. It was not there. But the plumping-mill crossbar was. Frightful alighted on it.

"Creee, creee, creee, car-reet." She was home.

Sam leaped from the rock and walked slowly toward her. His blue eyes looked into hers. His suntanned face creased with his big smile of wonder.

"Now, what do I do with you, beautiful bird?" he asked. "I can't keep you. The Feds say I'm not old enough to have a falconer's license." Frightful tipped her head and focused an eye on Sam.

"If I keep you, the Fish and Wildlife Service will just take you away from me. Maybe even jail me. You're an endangered species. I can't harbor an endangered species. I've learned that much!

"But," he said, leaning closer to her, "if I don't jess and leash you, you're not a captive bird.

"Will you stay anyway?"

Frightful made soft noises and flew to the Baron Weasel rock. The plumping-mill stick slipped and fell to the ground.

It hit with a force that scared Frightful. She flew to the lowest limb of the hemlock. Sam sat still.

"I missed you," he said. She lifted her feathers and softened her eyes. His words held the sounds she recognized as human love and affection. He chatted on.

"I'm pretty good at getting squirrels now, Frightful," he said. "I had to learn to hunt them after they took you from me. I use the same kind of sling David used to kill Goliath. It's accurate and packs a wallop. But it's not like hunting with you. We were a team, and we shared such good food. Tasty rabbit for you, rabbit stew for me; good pheasant liver for you, pheasant pot pie for me. Squirrels just don't quite make it."

Frightful bobbed her head and listened. Sam talked on.

"Alice and Mrs. Strawberry eat pork. Alice bred Crystal, her pet pig, and she and Mrs. Strawberry raised the piglets. They sold several of them for lots of money. They butchered one. It's pretty good. They saved three for breeders.

"I go down to the farm several times a week to help Mrs. Strawberry with her crops and garden. She can't do the heavy work anymore, and Alice is busy with the pigs and livestock. I like the work. I learn from the land and the sun and rain."

Frightful bent her knees to fly, but Sam spoke on, softly and rhythmically. She straightened up and listened.

"And Bando. Bando's making Adirondack furniture out of twisted forest saplings and limbs. They're wonderful pieces. People come from New York and far out of state to buy them.

"Zella's gotten so she likes their cabin. That is, after Bando and I got the waterwheel generating electricity. She has an electric stove and washing machine now. And—"

Footfalls in the woods alerted Frightful to danger, and she flew for the sky. Seconds later Alice came running up the path.

"Alice," Sam shouted. "Stay where you are."

"Why?"

"Frightful's here. You scared her." He circled the big hemlock, looking up among the limbs for his friend of the mountain.

"How do you know it's Frightful?" she asked.

"Creee, creee, creee, car-reet," Frightful called from overhead.

"Oh, Sam." Alice sucked in her breath and stared up at the hemlock. "It is Frightful. She called your name."

Frightful flashed her wings and flew over the trees.

Sam whistled the three notes, "Come to me," and ran to the bare rocks at the top of the mountain. He searched for her.

She was beyond his sight, cruising above the West Branch of the Delaware, looking for rats. She glided past the library and came to rest on the top of a handsome iron bridge. It was a bowstring truss seventy feet high. On each side of the span were iron bows. They were braced in place by a horizontal girder, to which iron columns and webs were riveted. The ends of the bows were embedded in cement pilings.

From the top of the downstream bow, Frightful saw the pigeons of Delhi. They wheeled up into the sky, broke apart, came together, and disappeared among the houses.

Frightful did not chase them. She had found the moun-

tain, she had found the tree, and she had found Sam. But a plumping mill was not a good perch. The bridge top was excellent. She dropped from the upper bow to the wide, horizontal girder.

She walked the girder until she came to a plate that joined the girder to the webbing. It was flat and roofed by the bow. She walked under it and looked out on the river and the valley. She liked this spot.

Frightful rested and pulled a foot into her breast feathers. The sun dropped low. Below her, red-winged blackbirds clinked good-night songs as they retired among the tall rushes. The cars that drove over the bridge trembled it as if they were wind in the trees. Some deep peregrine instinct told her this was where she belonged. Not in the forest. Not in a mews. She preened her feathers and watched the sun set. Night came.

In the morning she was hungry, very hungry. She flew up and down the river, saw nothing moving, and returned to the one hemlock.

"Creee, creee, creee, car-eet."

Sam burst through the deerskin door of the tree. He pulled on his deerskin jacket and waved his gloved hand.

"Okay," he called. "Let's go hunting, old friend." Whistling and swinging his arms, he ran down the trail to the meadow.

Frightful knew exactly where he was going and flew ahead of him to their old hunting ground. She waited on while Sam kicked through the weeds and grasses, still covered with snow. A rabbit jumped up, but so did a wood rat.

Frightful struck the rat. She covered it with her wings. The sky was full of thieves. Sam ran to her.

"Well, I'll be," he said. "A rat! Think I'm going to eat rat?" He laughed as he picked up both rat and Frightful in his gloved hand.

"Well, I'm not," he said. "You've got the whole thing to yourself." He smiled while Frightful ate. When she had consumed the parts she considered her share of food, she stopped eating. Sam took the food from her, and she rode home on his fist, free and unjessed. He talked happily to her.

"This might work," he said. "Both of us free."

As they approached the hemlock forest, Frightful looked up. Chup was overhead. She recognized his wing beat and shape. She opened her wings and flew from Sam's fist.

"Creee, creee, creee," she called.

"Thanks for the rat, Frightful," Sam called, but she was out of earshot. Still talking to her, he held up the rodent by the tail. "And just what do I do with this? Huh, Frightful? Pâté de rat?"

Wings rustled, talons dropped like a jet's landing gear, and a red-tailed hawk snagged the rat. She flew off.

"Well, that answers that," he said. "As Bando always says, 'Ask nature questions, and you will get answers.' "

Sam strode home over a forest floor spangled with flowering partridgeberry plants. He whistled and smiled.

Frightful maneuvered bumpy winds as she descended to the river and her bridge. She landed on the bow with a soft thud and looked up. Chup was flying straight to the cliff above the Schoharie River. She called. He heard but did not turn back. He was a smart missile aimed for a predetermined destination. Every March for ten years he had made this plunge from high above Sam's mountain to his aerie on the cliff.

Just before he flew over the road to Roxbury, a crew of

men in orange vests loaded equipment onto a yellow tractor-trailer. The materials had lain all winter at the end of Jon's road. A crane operator drove his awkward-looking vehicle off the grass onto the macadam and waited for instructions.

"The Margaretville Bridge is next," Joe Cassini, the foreman, said. "Then Delhi."

Although Frightful knew where Chup had gone, she did not follow him to the Schoharie cliff. Like many birds, the birds of prey mate for life, but Frightful had two forces keeping her where she was—Sam and the iron plate under the arc of the bowstring bridge. In a very few hours the bridge had become her aerie. It was home. And up the river on the mountaintop was Sam. She could hunt with him when she could not find food on her own.

Not only did her love for the iron plate and Sam keep her from going to Chup, but so did a new feeling deep inside her. She wanted to lie down. She scratched the plate with her talons several times, then lowered herself to her breast. She got up and scratched again. Frightful was making a scrape, a peregrine falcon's nest, which is nothing but bare earth or, in Frightful's case, an iron plate where she wanted to sit.

The more she scraped, the more content she became with her aerie, and the more Duchess, Lady, and Drum returned to her visual mind. That night she slept on her breast. She had never done that before.

The next day Frightful took inventory of the food of

Delhi. Pigeons were bountiful, and there would soon be more. Pairs were nesting in the rococo architecture of the churches and Victorian houses. Males and females took turns brooding the eggs and flying to the courthouse park to feast on seeds and bread. The food was scattered by two elderly sisters, who argued every day about which pigeon liked which sister the best.

That morning Frightful watched the ladies open their bags and scatter the food on the ground. A flock that had been waiting for the two women to arrive winged down from trees and cupolas, fighting each other for first place. Frightful caught a loser in midair. She carried it back to her iron aerie and stood over it. She did not eat it. She was waiting for the "psee" cry of baby falcons, or the "good girl, help yourself" words from Sam. Hearing neither, she finally ate.

That afternoon Frightful toured the backyards, the tumbling buildings in town, and dumps at its edges. Rats moved in and out of bags and boxes and auto parts. She saw whiskers twist, eyes move. When the rodents saw her, they disappeared deep in the debris.

Frightful circled wider, looking down on fields and farms beyond town. Female cottontails were preparing nests in the snow-matted grasses. There would soon be an abundance of young, and the young would have young. When they were all rushing around fighting for the limited food supply, Frightful would find them easy to catch. Like all predators, Frightful hunted the most abundant prey. She would take them until the rewards were not worth the energy spent to find and catch them. Then she would move on to other large populations, leaving the survivors to multiply.

Frightful returned to her bridge in the late afternoon. She walked along the broad horizontal girder, feeling in sync with her world. There was an abundance of food in and around Delhi. With Sam's and Jon's training, she had become a peregrine falcon of the twenty-first century. Her native taste for ducks and shorebirds had been replaced by an appetite for the pests of humankind.

She was hardly back from her tour when Chup flew over the bridge. He called to her. He cut love arcs before her eyes. She flew out to meet him. She spiraled in a sky roll with him. She copied his aerial loop-the-loop, then flew in tandem with him down the river. She was following closely when Chup suddenly sped toward the Schoharie River. Frightful followed reluctantly.

Over Gilboa, she braked by pulling down on her secondary flight feathers and tail. Turning in the air, she caught a northeasterly wind and went back to the West Branch of the Delaware. She skimmed up to and lit on the graceful bow of the Delhi Bridge.

In the late afternoon she grew very hungry and flew up the river to Sam's mountain and the one hemlock. She worked her way down through its dense limbs almost to the ground. Her old perch was back up. She hopped down onto it.

"Creee, creee, creee, car-reet," she called.

Sam poked his head out of the stone water mill he had built with the help of Bando and his wife, Zella, Alice, and the town's public librarian, Miss Turner. Bando looked out, too.

"Did I hear right?" Bando asked Sam.

"Yes, you did. Frightful's back. And," he said, "she's sitting on her perch."

"Desdemondia," Bando gasped, and grinned.

"Yesterday we hunted together. Just like old times," Sam said.

"She hunted with you?" Bando loved rabbit stew.

"Don't get excited; she hunts rats now."

"Rats?"

"Got any good recipes for rats?" Sam asked.

"Hmm," Bando said. "The wildest of all our falcons, the one most intolerant of human beings, has discovered rats. She will be an enormous asset to Delhi."

"Well, she's not helping me," said Sam. "I'm not going to eat rats."

Sam and Bando walked to the round stumps Sam had cut from the bole of a tree and sat down to watch Frightful.

"Wonder where she's been," Bando whispered. "Do you think she went south?"

"She looks as if she's been living in a palace," Sam answered in a low voice. "Her feathers, her posture, her demeanor say she's in wonderful condition."

"She came back to you," mused Bando. "That must mean she is imprinted on you—thinks you're her kind of critter. She probably won't mate."

"I'm not sure just how deeply she is imprinted on me," Sam said. "I got her when she was ten days old. Frightful knew her parents. That's not like the falcons that were incubated and nurtured from day one by people. They never mate with their kind. Frightful has a good chance to discover she is a peregrine falcon, find a fine mate, and have young."

"That'd be nice," said Bando. "Imagine having Frightfuls flying above the mountains and rivers of the Catskills again."

The two friends lapsed into silence. Bando leaned on the stone table; Sam wrapped his arms around his knees.

"She's back," mused Bando.

"I hope she mates," Sam said. "We sure need peregrine falcons. They're so important in the balance of nature."

The silver rays of twilight slanted through the hemlock needles in dusty streams. The kinglets, who were just back from the south, sang their vespers. Frightful was quiet. Sam and Bando were quiet.

Presently Frightful flew from her perch, wove her way up through the dense tree limbs to open sky, and returned to her bridge. She walked to her scrape. As night came to the Catskill Mountains, she pulled one foot into her breast feathers and closed her eyes.

The lengthening hours of daylight worked their spring magic on the birds. Their reproductive organs responded to the light, and they began to build nests. For her part, Frightful slept on her scrape, her breast against the iron plate. Despite blasts of cold winds, rain, and snow, Frightful felt the peregrine falcon spring.

She awoke at dawn to hear Lady calling and glanced up. Lady was headed home to the cliff above the Schoharie River where she had been raised. She had survived the winter in the traditional peregrine way by migrating to South America. She had lived on ducks and shorebirds, and she had ingested DDT. Banned by the U.S. Congress because it killed millions of birds, fish, and amphibians after World War II, the insecticide called DDT was still being used in South America. Lady got her share of the poison when she ate the birds who had eaten the DDT-killed insects in Chile. Each winter she would accumulate more of the poison in her body tissues. The shells of her eggs would be thin and eventually smash when she tried to incubate them. She would not live to be ten or twenty-five years old, as some peregrine falcons do. She would tremble and die after a few winters in South America.

Frightful watched Lady until she was out of sight. She did not see her come down on a sycamore tree near the

Margaretville Bridge. Men in orange coveralls were working there. Standing on platforms, they were painting the webs and cords sage green. A cement mixer churned. This was no place for nervous Lady.

She took off for the Schoharie River. Near her birthplace she flew into Chup. Recognizing her, he chased her away. Offspring do not come home. Lady sped east. When she had put forty miles between herself and her first home, she was over the upper Hudson River. Swinging back and forth across the great waterway, she searched for a cliff like the one she had been raised on.

No sooner was Lady out of sight than Frightful forgot her. She flew up and down the river, looping and spiraling; finally she turned and flew to Sam's mountain. She alighted on her perch. Sam was building a fire to cook his breakfast of wild cereal grains he had collected.

"Creee, creee, creee, car-reet."

He straightened up, saw Frightful, and his eyes twinkled.

"Good morning, beautiful bird," he said, taking her measure. "Guess we won't hunt today. You're fat and full of rat."

"Creee," she called softly.

After eating his porridge, Sam got a bowl he had chipped out of stone and filled it with chunks of pine resin. He put it in his stone oven and threw on more wood. The resin melted; he dipped a stick into the goo and worked it into a crack in the plumping-mill box. When it cooled, he poured water in it. The box no longer leaked.

Frightful looked out at nothing as she listened to old, familiar sounds on the mountain. Behind her the downy woodpecker drilled into a dead tree with a special beat she recognized. He had been a resident of the hemlock grove ever since she had lived there. A flock of ruby-crowned kinglets alighted in the top of the big hemlock. They called to each other a twittering farewell, as they did every year at this time. Sam's mountain was their last rendezvous on their trip north. From this forest they would fly off by twos to their ancestral breeding grounds.

"The kinglets are here," Sam said to Frightful. "It's bird springtime in the Catskills, snow and all." He looked up at the walnut-sized birds flitting among the tree limbs.

"Time to build a nest, Frightful," he called.

Frightful stretched one beautifully gray-spangled blue wing, then the other. Bending her knees, she pushed off and wove awkwardly upward through the trees. She was no forest goshawk.

Clear of the last twigs, she trilled a soft tribute to wings and flight, and dove freestyle down the mountain to the river. She was leveling off to land on the bridge when a male peregrine joined her. They landed simultaneously on the top of the arch of the bowstring truss.

"Chep, chep, chep," he called. Frightful jumped down

to the large horizontal web and walked to her scrape. He followed for a few steps, then stopped. Frightful was a third larger than he. He bowed to show his respect. An aluminum Fish and Wildlife Service band ringed his leg. He had been raised in captivity and released to the wild by Heinz Meng. The number 426 was visible on his band.

Frightful looked at him. She did not attack. He held a tasty bite of food in his beak and presented it to her. She accepted it. He bowed again, then shook out his feathers, which were ruffled and bent from travel. 426 had spent the winter in Ecuador and was now looking for a roost like the one he had known in the breeding barn of the falconer. Coming over Sam's mountain, he had seen Frightful and followed her to her aerie.

The coming of spring was affecting Frightful. She glanced at 426, leaned down, and scraped the iron plate. 426 came closer.

She lifted her feathers to him. He hurtled himself into the air, bulleted down the river valley, made a two-circle loop, climbed, and sped back to the bridge. Frightful watched his spectacular sky dance twice more, then she flew off the bridge and traced the same design in the air. She climbed, looped, and finally, in a graceful maneuver, held on to his feet as he flew upside down beneath her.

For three days Frightful and 426 danced above the river and mountains. They flew so high they could see the Hudson River. They flew so low they scared the nesting red-wings. Upside down, they called to each other.

Then Frightful led 426 to the one mountain.

"Creee, creee, creee, car-reet," she called, and landed in the hemlock tree. 426 came down beside her.

Sam whistled their hunting tune.

Frightful left 426 and flew to the mountain meadow. There she waited on, watching Sam run through the laurel and seedling hemlocks to their field. Just as he arrived, 426 swooped under her, took her feet in his, and swung her in an arc up into the sky. High above Sam they opened their wings and flew in tandem down the mountain over the river, up into the clouds and back to Sam.

Laughing, crying, Sam watched them disappear again.

"Frightful, you've got a mate!" he exclaimed, and climbed the nearest tree as swiftly as a marten. Near the top he saw Frightful and 426 drop out of sight in the river valley. Suddenly they reappeared again and, looping side by side, flew straight toward Delhi.

Sam noted their direction. He lined up the top tree on a mountain with the weather-vane rooster on the peak of a distant barn and scrambled down.

He ran full speed downhill for the West Branch of the Delaware, looking at rocks and trees for white streaks of bird excrement that marked a peregrine falcon aerie. He saw no such marks, absolutely none, then remembered that Leon Longbridge had told him no peregrine falcon would nest near Delhi—no cliffs. The bridge was high, and he recalled that peregrines had learned to nest on bridges. Running hard, he took his Peaks Brook trail to town.

When Sam reached the bridge, Frightful was playing with 426, sliding and gliding on the winds at fifteen hundred feet.

Finding no telltale marks of an aerie on the bridge, Sam walked up Elm Street and stopped in the library to get a book on farming wild edible plants. He was returning when Frightful and 426 came back to the bridge. She saw Sam. He did not see her, and she did not call his name.

It was evening. Eighteen miles and sixteen minutes away as the falcon flies, the repair work on the Margaretville Bridge was nearing completion. Supplies were loaded onto trucks and flatbeds, and orders were called in for air compressors and movable work platforms.

"The bowstring bridge at Delhi is next," Joe Cassini said on a cellular phone to his boss at the Department of Transportation in Albany.

The following dawn the sky was pink and orange with May's morning light. Frightful and 426 mated. Fifty hours later she retired to the scrape. Sitting down, the wind from the river brushing her face, she laid a pale cream-and-pink egg. It was mottled with rich red-and-brown splotches. Thousands of tiny pores in the shell allowed oxygen to enter and water and carbon dioxide to escape. A thin cuticle glistened on its surface. This would prevent bacteria from getting through the shell. The egg was a masterpiece.

Frightful did not incubate it. She and 426 perched nearby, looking at it and feeling new interest in the bridge and the river valley. Then they took off together, a synchronized pair, looping and diving in the sky.

IN   WHICH
There Are Eggs and Trouble

Two days later Frightful laid a second egg. Again she did not incubate it. Without her warmth, the embryos could not develop. Nevertheless they needed attention, and she turned them every three or four hours. The turning twisted the ropelike chalzas attached to each end of the yolk and to the shell. This twisting tightened the chalzas and kept the yolks suspended in the middle of the albumen so that they did not stick to the inner shell.

Frightful pulled a feather from her breast and watched it blow off on a wind. Before she lay the first egg, both she and 426 had lost so many feathers on their breasts that these areas were naked and bare. These were brood patches.

Both parents would brood the eggs. Warmer than feathers, the bare skin would raise the eggs to seventy degrees Fahrenheit. At that mystical temperature, life would start.

The day Frightful laid the second egg was cold. Nevertheless, she and 426 left the eggs and flew off to the courthouse cupola. 426 saw the pigeon ladies come out of their house and the pigeons flock to meet them. He dove. The pigeons scattered. Frightful watched from above the trees. She saw a bird fly away from the others in confusion, dove at it, and missed.

Later that day they were successful in their cooperative hunting. Frightful caught a rat.

That night was very cold. Frightful stood over the eggs, not sitting on them to start incubation, but protecting them from the freezing air. She let her long breast feathers and pantaloons make a tent around them as she stood. Her brood patch was swollen and soft with a jellylike fluid.

Three days after the second egg was laid, Frightful laid a third. When she stood up to look at the rich colors and exciting shapes of her clutch, her knees bent. She sat down. Her brood patch fit gently around the eggs like a soft hot-water bottle. Long feathers that had developed around her brood patch dropped around the eggs like a down comforter. They kept the warmth in and the cold out.

Around noon the peregrine eggs reached seventy degrees. Miraculously, inside each egg one cell became two,

two became four, then eight. Life was exploding in its various and complicated ways. Frightful sat tight.

That afternoon 426 became provider and helper. He flew off alone and came back with food. He fed her, then she stood up. He sat down and brooded the eggs. Frightful flew up and down the river, then winged over the one hemlock, calling to Sam. When she was well exercised, she returned to the scrape. 426 got up. Frightful sat down on the precious eggs.

Around six o'clock the next morning 426, who was sleeping near the top of the bridge against a vertical web, awoke. He checked Frightful and flew off to hunt.

Sam saw him go. He walked onto the bridge and whistled. Frightful did not answer.

"I know you're there," he said. "I've been watching you from Federal Hill."

Frightful was quiet. The longer she incubated, the more deeply she went into the trance of incubation. Only 426 could bring her out of it, and only to eat and fly briefly.

Sam whistled again. Still no answer. He grinned. Frightful, he knew, was now incubating.

"Good girl," he said aloud; then to himself, "At last I know for sure that she is not so deeply imprinted on me that she could not mate and raise eyases. I am so, so glad. I did not destroy her wildness after all."

Whistling, Sam swung off the bridge and dropped to the water's edge, where he walked gracefully upriver, jumping stones and skirting marshes. He arrived at the path to Mrs. Strawberry's farm. Today was the day to plant her rye. The maple leaves were flowering.

On May 8 a diesel truck, pulling a flatbed of lumber and roadblocks, crossed the Delhi Bridge and parked on the town side of the river. Workmen placed detour signs and orange cones on either end of the bridge, tied orange ribbons to webs, and conferred with their boss, Joe Cassini.

The café owner, Betty Christopher, drove up in her car and poked her head out the window.

"What's all this about?" she asked Joe Cassini.

"Bridge repair," he answered.

"About time," she said. "The last couple of floods just about tore out the pilings. Gonna fix them, too?"

"Yeah," Cassini answered. "The pilings are first."

"I've been expecting them to go any day," said Betty Christopher, "and dump everyone on the bridge into the river. I'm glad you're here."

"They're not that bad," laughed Joe Cassini. "But we're repairing this bridge and every other bridge in New York State. Even ones that hardly need it."

"How am I going to get to work?" she asked. "I live on the mountain side of the bridge, not the town side."

"We're setting up a detour. Turn around and cross on the lower bridge."

"Gotcha," she said, and drove off.

A week later the workmen finished the crib that would

support the bridge while they replaced the pilings. No sooner was it up than a diesel truck with air compressors pulled onto the bridge. Men with ear protectors picked up their jackhammers and tested them. Blasts shook the bridge.

Frightful stood up.

"There's a peregrine's nest on this bridge." It was Sam's voice below. She sat down.

"So?" said Joe Cassini.

"Well, peregrines are an endangered species," he said. "They are protected by law."

"We ain't going to shoot them," Joe Cassini said.

"But you'll scare them away," Sam replied. "Isn't there another bridge you could work on till the end of June?"

"There are a lot of other bridges. But the Department of Transportation says we do this one—now."

"Tell them peregrine falcons are nesting here. I'm sure when they hear that, they'll want to wait until the nesting season is over. These are very special birds."

"You tell them," Joe Cassini said. "I don't know anything about that stuff." He gave orders to a man who was standing beside the piling and turned his back on Sam.

Sam looked up at the long horizontal girder, then down at his body. He measured his body width against the width of the girder.

"It ought to work," he said, and ambled toward the mountain side of the bridge. Walking to the bottom of the bow, he glanced back. The repair crew was busy. Grabbing the bow in both hands, he ran up it like a spider. At the fifth vertical from the mountain shore, he eased onto the wide horizontal girder and lay down. He was out of sight on his belly. He inchwormed to Frightful. She was tucked under the bow, her eyes calm and broody. Sam pressed his lips together and chirped.

"Car-reet," Frightful answered, and stood up. She turned the eggs to keep the developing embryos from sticking to the shells.

Leon Longbridge, the conservation officer, and four kids walked onto the bridge. Sam watched Leon. A little less than a year ago Sam had thought Leon Longbridge was the man who had confiscated Frightful and taken her from him. Sam had been dead wrong. The culprit was a falcon thief named Bate. Leon Longbridge was Delhi's conservation officer and a truly fine man, as the town kids had discovered. Leon's favorite bird was the peregrine falcon, and last summer when a boy named José Cruz and a girl named Molly came to his office to ask about peregrine falcons, he had expounded with beautiful stories about their courage and swiftness. They wanted to hear more, and it was not long before he found himself taking them on early-morning bird walks.

Only last evening, Molly, who was ten years old with black bangs and a pigtail, had called him.

"I think two peregrine falcons are nesting on the bridge," she had said. "And the workers are scaring them."

"Good for you," he had said. "You're right. There is a pair on the bridge, and I am sure all the noisy equipment will drive them away. I'm going to ask the foreman if he can't work somewhere else the first thing in the morning."

"Can José and I come with you?" she had asked.

"Sure," he had said.

"And Maria and Hughie?"

"I don't see why not," he had answered. "The more the better."

Now Sam, flattened out on the girder, was watching them walk toward the foreman.

"Off the bridge," Joe Cassini shouted. "The bridge is closed. Get off."

"Peregrine falcons are nesting on this bridge," Molly piped.

"We've come to ask if you could stop work," Leon Longbridge said. "Could you work somewhere else for a month or so?"

"Get off the bridge," Joe repeated. Leon Longbridge nodded and led the kids to the riverbank.

"Let's hold a meeting," Molly said, and sat down on the grass.

Leon told them the endangered species were protected by the federal government. He said he had notified the U.S. Fish and Wildlife Service in Albany that the birds were in trouble. The Feds seemed to think the birds would be all right.

"Anyone know the governor?" Leon asked. "He can stop the repairs."

"Not me," said José, and slapped his black, curly head with both hands. "I wish I did."

"By the way, Molly," Leon asked, "how did you happen to see the falcons?"

"My bedroom looks out on the bridge," she said, and pointed to a Victorian masterpiece at the bottom of the mountain, directly in line with the bridge.

"What can we do?" said Maria, a sturdy little girl in white overalls. "The workers are going to scare them away."

"What about writing letters to the governor?" Molly asked.

"Yeah," said José. "When Jon Wood showed us a peregrine falcon that had been electrocuted on utility poles, we wrote letters to the company."

"And they fixed three poles," said Molly.

"Move on," Joe Cassini called. "It's dangerous here."

"Let's go back to my office," said Leon, getting to his feet. "I have papers and pencils there."

As they jumped to their feet and hurried off, a crew member put on his ear protectors, picked up his jackhammer, and pushed the start button. The powerful tool roared. He attacked the piling, the jackhammer shaking and spewing dust. The noise bounced off one hundred iron webs in an earsplitting exchange of sounds.

The kids and Leon Longbridge looked back to see the falcon fly in terror. She did not.

Stretched on his belly, Sam spoke gently to Frightful.

The constant vibrations from two jackhammers trembled the huge horizontal web, but Frightful stayed with her eggs. When two more hammers joined the mayhem, she came out of her incubation trance. Her eyes widened in fear.

"Pseee," Sam called, squeezing air between his teeth to make a bird sound.

Frightful stood up.

Softly, softly Sam whistled to her. She cocked her head. The jackhammers stopped. She did not fly.

"Car-reet."

"It's all right," Sam said. "It's all right."

He reached out his hand to her.

The four jackhammers blasted again, sending sound waves bouncing around the webs and girders that held the bows in place. The waves banged out every possible note known to iron and air.

"Car-reet," Frightful called softly.

Sam lay perfectly still, his hand inches from her. Relaxed and smiling, he whispered over and over, "It's all right, Frightful. It's all right."

She pressed the precious eggs against her warm brood patch. She settled down but was still alert.

For the three hours that the jackhammers blasted, Frightful watched Sam. He transmitted calmness. Despite the din, she slipped into the trance of incubation, this time more deeply than before. She saw and heard nothing beyond her scrape.

At twelve o'clock the work crew put down their tools and ambled to the river's edge to eat their brown-bag lunches. The bridge was quiet.

Sam stood up, touched his toes, and stretched. He backed up against the next vertical iron web to keep out of sight of the workers and glanced at the river far below.

"I feel like a bird way up here," he said to Frightful. "What a super thing it must be to fly."

Frightful did not stir.

426 dropped out of the mist of a low cumulus cloud, where he had been nervously circling. He landed on the top of the bow with food for Frightful. He saw Sam and flexed his legs to take off, but did not. 426 had been hacked to the wild by a motherly human. If frightful was at ease with Sam, so was he. Sam did not move a finger.

426 shifted the bird in his talons to his beak, and dropped down to Frightful. He called the peregrine note to awaken a mate from the incubation trance. Frightful brightened and looked at him. Glancing at Sam, who was tree still, he tore off a bite and presented it to Frightful.

A jackhammer blasted. 426 swallowed the offering and took off in panic. Frightful was ready to follow him. But the eggs had power over her. Feeling them beneath her, she settled back to mother them.

"Frightful," Sam said. "This is going to be a problem. 426 is not going to feed you with those blasters around." He took his penknife from his pocket and cut off tender bites. Frightful took the food from him until she was satiated.

"I wish you could exercise," he said. "I can feed you, but I sure can't sit on the eggs."

At five o'clock the noise ended. The work crew drove away, and Sam got to his feet.

"You're a brave bird," he said. "Hang in there. I'm going to catch and cook me a fish.

"Then I'm going to make a camouflage. Somebody is

going to look up here, and if they are standing at the right angle, they'll see me. With a burlap bag and some reeds woven into it, they'll think I'm windblown debris.

"When I go down, I'll leave it up here. Hopefully all the falcon watchers will think it's the nest.

"And something else. I'll get Alice to buy some orange material. She and Mrs. Strawberry can make a vest I'll wear, like the workers. There's a hard hat in Mrs. Strawberry's barn. If anyone sees me climbing up the bow to the nest, they'll think I'm a crew member." He looked down on the broody Frightful. "You and I have got to get these little birds in the sky. The rivers and valleys need them."

He whistled softly.

"Sleep well. I'll be back in the morning."

IN WHICH
The Kids Are Heard

For fifteen days Frightful, with Sam's help, sat through the blasts of the jackhammers and the rumble of trucks. 426 bravely brought food to her at noon when the bridge was quiet, but he could not drive himself to take his turn brooding.

But he did not abandon his family. He watched Frightful during the day from the big sycamore tree on the riverbank and at night from the top of the bridge.

Frightful slowly adjusted to the noise of the jackhammers. Sam was nearby. She listened to his soft whistles and words when the noise was the worst. 426 was too terrified to come to the nest and feed her, but he dropped food onto the girder. Sam took his place and fed it to her.

Each day as she felt the chicks develop, Frightful heard less of the commotion.

On day eighteen of incubation, Joe Cassini looked up and noticed sticks and reeds where the fifth vertical met the bow.

"There's that nest everyone's so riled up about," he said to Dan Martin, a Mohawk Indian whose balance and fearlessness on high girders made him one of the most valuable bridge workers. "Looks perfectly fine to me."

Dan studied the sticks.

"Yeah," he said. "Messy bird." Then he thought a minute. "I never knew peregrine falcons made nests. They like bare ground."

"I guess we learn something every day," said Joe Cassini.

Dan Martin wasn't convinced. He kept an eye on the nest as he carried lumber to the men who were building a form around the ravaged piling. As he worked, he wondered about a peregrine falcon and a stick nest.

On day twenty the jackhammers stopped. The cement mixer drove onto the bridge, and blasts were replaced by grinding and tumbling sounds. Frightful barely heard them.

She could feel the chicks move inside the eggs. The yolks had transformed into embryos, complete with tiny blood vessels, and they had grown heavier. This sent her deeper into the incubation trance. Even a dynamite blast on day twenty-two did not frighten her.

With the jackhammers silent, 426 fed Frightful again and nervously sat down and brooded the eggs while she exercised. Sam watched, ready to help out if 426 became frightened again.

One day when the tiercel was brooding the eggs and Frightful was looping and gliding, she heard Sam whistle from the mountain that rose above the river. The three-note call had a new ending, a "yippee" note that said, "All is well."

Sam was in a lean-to he had constructed on the mountainside. It was eye level with Frightful's aerie. Out from it he fished and gathered wild tubers and greens. After dinner he would lean back against the base of an old chestnut oak, put his hands under his head, and watch the aerie. Now and then he whistled to Frightful.

On this evening Frightful answered his call with "carreet," and he smiled and remembered how she had saved his life by catching food for him in the wilderness.

"We'll get through this, too, old girl," he said. "Only nine days to go."

When the sun set that night, Sam cut one more notch in

a stick to keep track of the thirty-one days of incubation. He wondered why Leon Longbridge had not been successful in stopping the repairs. Leon wondered why the birds had not deserted. Relentlessly, the bridge work went on.

Sam now went up the iron bowstring bridge to feed Frightful only if the equipment on the bridge indicated it was going to be another noisy day. 426 had not adjusted to that. On these days Sam climbed to Frightful before the kids came by on their way to school to check on the falcons. They would look, smile, and leave a little before the school bell rang and the work crew arrived. In this interval Sam had time to climb down the bridge and disappear without being seen.

One morning when Sam had finished feeding Frightful and was on his way down, Molly arrived. She saw him. Quickly he stepped to the horizontal girder and walked to the middle of the bridge, his orange vest catching the sunlight. He inspected the bolts in the web joints and made notes without pencil or paper. Then he turned and walked past the nest, grabbed the iron bow, and backed down to the bridge floor. With Molly still looking at him, he dropped over the bridge, grabbed the form around the piling, and climbed down to the river shore. He vanished in the cattails.

That day, as Sam had anticipated, was an extremely noisy one. 426 stayed away, and Sam didn't get back to Frightful until after five. She was ravenously hungry. He fed her until her crop was full. Satisfied, she arose and turned the eggs.

The next morning just after Sam arrived, Frightful heard the voice of her winter friend, Jon Wood. He was on the bridge with Leon Longbridge. The two had been consulting about how to save the peregrines of the Delhi Bridge.

"We aren't getting anywhere with the Department of Transportation," Jon said. "They won't stop the work for any reason at all. None."

"That's what the Department of Wildlife Conservation is telling me, too," said Leon Longbridge. "My boss has been trying to stop them; but the order is—make these bridges safe. The Feds don't think it's a problem yet."

"I had hoped the kids' letters would get some action," Jon said. "They got the utility company to fix several poles. Molly told me they've written the governor about the peregrines. He controls the Department of Transportation."

"Yeah," said Leon Longbridge, "but they are only getting form letters back; 'thank you, but . . .' " He studied the aerie.

"I think we ought to move the eggs," Jon finally said. "She's been incubating long enough to be so deeply attached to them that she'll follow them anywhere. We can put a box in that sycamore tree by the river and transfer the eggs to it. She ought to go right to them."

"I know songbirds will go to nestlings when you move

them," Leon said. "But I've had no experience with moving eggs."

"Well," said Jon, "sometimes it works, sometimes it doesn't. Let's give her a few more days. She seems to have adjusted."

"I just can't believe the female didn't leave the first day the work crew blasted off their jackhammers," Leon said. "She had hardly finished laying. Most females would have deserted this nest and found another site. She had plenty of time to lay again."

"Something we don't understand is holding her there," Jon said.

When the first workers arrived, Jon and Leon left the bridge.

"I don't get it," Jon said, shaking his head. "Peregrine falcons—two of the mere thirty-four in the entire state— and the bureaucrats won't stop this work for them."

"NASA held back on a rocket launch to save a nest of egrets," said Leon. "But New York can't save endangered falcons."

They walked to their cars in silence.

"By the way," Leon said as he unlocked his door, "tomorrow before school the kids are going to hold a parade to save the falcons."

"That's great," Jon said. "But they'd be more effective in Albany."

"I don't think anything will change Albany," Leon said. "The orders to go forward with the repairs are written in stone."

Jon looked up at the bridge.

"At least the jackhammers have stopped," he said. "The Transportation Department said it would only take a few more days to finish pouring the cement for the pilings. Then we can relax if . . . if she's still there."

"I think we ought try to move her," said Leon. "I made a scrape—an open box with a narrow strip of wood to keep the eggs from rolling out. I'll put sand on the bottom."

"Hmm," said Jon, glancing up at the aerie.

"Can you help me put the box in that big sycamore?" Leon asked. "I think we ought to try something."

Jon started his van. "I still can't believe the female hasn't deserted," he said. "Only that serene falcon Susan named Destiny would put up with this."

Suddenly he jumped out of the van and lifted his binoculars to his eyes. "Hmm," he said to himself. "She did fly toward Delhi. Hmm."

Leon studied the aerie again.

"There are sticks near the nest," he said. "They've been there for about two weeks. What do you make of that?"

"I have no idea," Jon said. "Sometimes the tiercel will bring a stick or two to his mate out of love, but not that many—I don't think. Still, there must be some explana-

tion. There are a lot of mysterious things about that nest."
He shook his head, got back into his car, and drove off.

Sam was stretched out on the wide girder, under the
burlap camouflage. The cool air from the river had carried
the voices of Jon and Leon to his ears.

He had not expected anyone to question the sticks and
reeds. When he looked at them from the ground, he could
believe that either a tiercel had brought them or maybe even
an osprey. The big fish hawks put sticks in many places
during the breeding season. Suddenly he was worried.
Maybe, he thought, it really is time to move Frightful and
her eggs. If they don't, I will.

Belly flat on the girder, he watched the workers pick up
their equipment and put on their hard hats. When they
were busy, he slipped out from under the burlap and
straightened his orange vest. He pulled himself to the bow
and backed down to the bottom like a veteran engineer. No
one paid any attention to him. He walked off to his lean-to
and removed his vest and hard hat.

Before sunrise the next day, Sam hurried down-
mountain to the big sycamore, jumped for the lowest limb,
and swung hand over hand to the trunk. He climbed, ex-
amining limbs and forks. When he could go no farther he
whistled to Frightful. They were about eye level.

"Creee, creee, creee, car-reet," she answered wistfully,
and stood up then, turned her eggs.

"How do you like this spot?" he asked. She was brooding again.

He was about to climb down when he saw kids gathering at the public library. They were waving handmade posters. Hughie Smith, the middle-school drummer, beat his drum, and the poster carriers strode down Elm Street, headed for the bridge.

PEREGRINES EAT RATS.
SAVE OUR TOWN.

PEREGRINES ARE NOBLE.
WAIT ONE MONTH TO REPAIR
THE BRIDGE.

IT TAKES ONLY THIRTY-ONE DAYS
FOR A BABY FALCON TO HATCH.
IT TOOK MILLIONS OF YEARS
TO MAKE THE FALCONS.
STOP THE BRIDGE REPAIRS.
SAVE THE PEREGRINES.

WE HAVEN'T FALLEN IN THE RIVER YET.
POSTPONE THE BRIDGE REPAIRS.
LET THE FALCONS RAISE THEIR YOUNG.

SAVE THE PEREGRINE. SAVE US.
WE ARE NATURE, TOO.

By the time the parade reached the Delhi Bridge, there were about thirty youngsters. Beaming parents and curious townspeople stood on the sidewalks, watching.

Joe Cassini had been warned about the parade and had come to work early. He stepped out to meet the protesters.

"Go on home or you'll be arrested," he said, shooing the kids away with gestures.

Molly stepped forward, trembling but determined.

"We just want you to stop repairing the bridge until the end of June," she piped.

José was emboldened by her courage. "That's all the time the falcons need to grow up and fly away."

Hughie beat out a roll on the drum.

Cassini crossed his arms on his chest. "Go home," he repeated.

"I can't believe you don't care," said Molly, backing away. "These are endangered falcons. And they are going to have babies."

"It ain't my decision," the foreman stated firmly. "Orders come from Albany. Tell them."

"We did," said Maria Carlos, who was wearing a peregrine T-shirt she had designed. "They don't see any problem."

"Neither do I," said Cassini. "The bird is still up there, isn't she? We haven't scared her off. What's the big deal? Now, get going." He walked toward them.

"No," said Molly.

Leon Longbridge came running up to her.

"Come on, Molly. This way, Hughie," he said. "Let's go into town. We'll march down Main Street."

Glad for the suggestion, the kids turned around and walked up Elm Street to Main. Cars slowed; pedestrians stopped. Parents confessed to strangers and each other that they never had the least interest in falcons until their children told them about the peregrines of the Delhi Bridge. They were furious that the state wouldn't stop work until the little birds got on wing. The crowd wasn't large, but the police chief recognized an awakening "situation" when he saw one. He called for more officers.

Then he led the parade to the park in front of the courthouse and let the falcon lovers wave their signs at passing cars.

"Save the peregrines," shouted José. A TV cameraman and a newswoman jumped out of a van, looked over the kids, and walked up to José.

"What is your name?" the newswoman asked, holding the mike close to his face.

"José Cruz, first baseman on the school team. I am ten years old and I am in the fifth grade. I want to grow up and become a falconer."

"Thank you. You've answered the first question fully. Now the big one."

"What is it?"

"Do you think it's more important to save a peregrine falcon nest or mend a dangerous bridge?"

"Save the peregrine falcons," José answered clearly. "Save the peregrine falcons!" a cluster of nearby kids echoed.

"But what about people? Aren't they important?"

"They have a detour," José said. "Save the peregrine falcons," he repeated. The other kids cheered and stuck their posters in front of the camera.

"Thank you very much," said the interviewer and turned to a jackhammer operator who had come to the park to fill his water bottle.

"How do you feel about this problem?" she asked.

"Save the peregrine falcons," he said in a loud, clear voice.

A gleeful roar went up from the poster wavers. Cars coming off the detour slowed and stopped. Horns blasted.

"What's going on?" an out-of-town driver asked.

"Keep moving, keep moving," ordered a police officer, stepping into the road and waving the car on. "You're backing up traffic. Keep moving."

The courthouse clock struck 8:30 A.M.

"School," said Molly. "Let's go." Hughie Smith rolled his drum, and the police officers stopped traffic to let the kids cross Main Street.

Sam, who was watching from the sycamore tree, decided this was a good time to feed Frightful. She hadn't eaten this morning.

He was pulling on his orange vest when 426 dropped out of the sky and lit on the aerie near the scrape. He bowed to Frightful and called the note that broke the incubation trance. She got off the eggs. He took her place—and brooded.

"Wow, good," Sam exclaimed. "We may get little chicks yet."

Sam returned to his mountainside camp and ate a breakfast of nuts and dried apples from his root cellar on the mountaintop.

Things continued to go well the next few days. The cement pouring ended. After that the noise level dropped to tolerable. A few days later Molly borrowed a spotting scope from the Audubon Club, and she and her friends set it up in her room with its perfect view of the nest. Frightful and the scrape filled the lens.

"They'll be hatching soon," Molly said, and let Hughie Smith take a look.

"It seems," he said with a wistful smile, "that despite everything, the peregrines of Delhi are going to have chicks." He turned and looked at Molly. "The mom is fidgety like a hen hatching eggs."

At that moment Frightful heard the chicks cheeping inside their shells. She listened, not hearing the workers below or Sam Gribley, who was creeping along the girder to her.

"Frightful," he said, disbelief in his voice. "Now they're going to paint the bridge!"

There Are Three

At dawn the next day Leon Longbridge wedged the wooden scrape into a fork in the sycamore tree and wired it in place. He climbed down and hurried to his car to watch what came next. Frightful was too broody to notice what was going on below her, but not 426. He sat on the bridge top in the cold dawn, watching Leon climb down from the tree and Jon Wood grab the iron bow and climb toward him.

When Jon was too close, 426 took off with a loud snap of his wings, climbed high, and dove at the man. Jon ducked and climbed on.

Sam in his lean-to was also watching.

"That ought to work," he said to himself. "The eggs are so close to hatching, she won't abandon them."

Frightful snapped out of her trance when Jon Wood swung down to the horizontal girder. She got to her feet.

"Hello, Destiny," he whispered. "I'd know you anywhere."

Frightful recognized him.

"Psee," she called, and stepped back over her eggs.

He inched slowly toward her.

426 screamed the alarm of the peregrine. The penetrating call touched Frightful's survival instinct, and she flew off the eggs.

The air was cold. Jon carefully wrapped the warm eggs in bubble plastic and lowered them onto a hot-water bottle in his backpack. He shouldered the pack, grabbed the bow, swung up onto it, and backed down its curved slope to the bridge.

Frightful flew back to her scrape. Her eggs were gone.

"Kek, kek, kek," she cried. 426 answered her distress

call and dropped down beside her. The empty nest stunned and confused them.

Movement at the foot of the sycamore caught Frightful's eye, and she saw Jon Wood. She screamed and dove. He was the one who had taken her eggs. He saw her coming and covered his head with his hands. A talon scraped him. Quickly he scaled the tree to the artificial scrape and, fending off Frightful with one arm, he gently lay the eggs in the box. He climbed down, ran across the bridge, and joined Leon Longbridge in his car.

Frightful circled and swooped to a limb in the sycamore tree. 426 joined her.

Sam watched. Leon and Jon watched.

Minutes passed. The air was cool.

Frightful flew from the tree back to the bridge. She circled once and flew back to the tree.

She cried her worried call.

426 answered. Agitated, he flew over the town. Frightful followed him.

An hour passed. The pair did not come back.

"Okay," said Jon Wood. "This isn't working. The eggs have been uncovered for sixty minutes, and at forty-five degrees Fahrenheit, that's not good. I'm going to put them back."

He climbed to the box, wrapped up the eggs once more, and returned them to the scrape on the bridge.

He was backing away when Frightful lit on the girder and, putting one foot in front of the other, ran to the eggs. She sat down and pressed her brood patch against them. She stood up. The eggs were cold. She sat down again.

An hour later she got up and walked away. The chicks in the shells had not moved. She walked back, turned, and snuggled them against her brood patch. She called wistfully.

Dan Martin arrived early for work. He looked up at the gray-blue sky and put on his rain gear. Seeing Leon Longbridge and Jon Wood, he asked about the falcons. Jon told him they had tried unsuccessfully to move the eggs.

"We've got to somehow postpone the bridge painting," Jon said. "I guess there is nothing you can do. I'll try calling Albany again."

The rain was beginning to fall when Joe Cassini arrived. Dan Martin greeted him as he got out of his car.

"We can't paint today," he said. "Bad rainstorm coming."

"We can sandblast," Joe Cassini said. "Is there any reason why we can't start cleaning up rust spots in the rain?"

"No," said Dan Martin. "Rain shouldn't make any difference."

Then Joe Cassini turned to Dan and put his hand on his shoulder.

"When we get to the webs," he said, "I want you to

paint the ones near the nest. You seem to know something about peregrine falcons."

"Enough to ask this: Do we still have to go ahead with the work? The bridge won't fall down now."

"We still have to go ahead," Joe Cassini said. "I checked with Albany myself. The governor is relentless. Said the tourists were beginning to come to the Catskills, and he wants the work done on time."

"I've just been talking to Leon Longbridge and Jon Wood," Dan Martin said. "They tried to move the eggs to another site this morning."

"Yeah?"

"It didn't work. They had to put them back before they froze."

Joe Cassini glanced at the aerie. "Funny," he said, "but I like those birds. They're real spunky."

Two hours later, when Frightful again turned the eggs, there was still no movement.

426 arrived with a pigeon. He pulled off a morsel to feed Frightful. The sandblasting machine started up. 426 dove onto his wings and sped away.

Sam left his lean-to and walked partway down the mountain. Frightful had not eaten for eleven hours. The high-pitched noise of the sanders had driven 426 away. The tiercel, he knew, wouldn't come back until the workers went home. And that was too late.

Frightful had to be fed, but how? The crewmen were all

over the bridge, hanging work platforms and blasting rust. There was no way he could climb to the aerie without being seen, and he did not want to be seen. Not now. He had worked with Frightful for two weeks, and he didn't want to be stopped. Best to keep out of sight. He was known in Delhi to a few people—Miss Turner, the librarian; Leon Longbridge; and some of the kids. They referred to him as Thoreau, the boy who lived on Peaks Brook Mountain. That was just fine, but climbing a bridge made him obvious, and that was something Sam didn't want.

Just before noon, the rain poured down in torrents. The crew got into their cars or ran to the café. Sam's deerskin jacket repelled water like a nor'easter coat. He lifted his binoculars.

Frightful was off the eggs. She was standing on the food 426 had brought, eating heartily. When she was satisfied, she brooded again.

"She must have brought the eggs back to temperature," he said. "Even in this rain. What a noble bird."

Sam walked down the mountain, crossed the river on rocks, and took the long trail to his hemlock tree. He lit a fire in his fireplace and stretched out on his bed.

"Four or five more days," he said. "I wonder what else can happen?"

At that moment Frightful felt the chicks move vigorously inside their shells. A burst of rain struck the bow and rushed down the vertical webs. Water spilled on her. She sat calmly, a tent over her precious eggs.

Day twenty-nine dawned cold. A snow flurry powdered the mountains and dropped white crystals on the town. Frightful cocked her head and stood up. One egg was vibrating. Inside, the chick's neck was twitching spasmodically, then its little body stiffened. A sharp egg tooth on the top of its beak pierced the inner membrane, and its nostrils pushed into the pocket of air at the top of the egg. The chick's lungs filled. It breathed.

"Cheep."

Frightful lifted her body so that she had very little weight on the hatching chick. Her warm feathers fell around it. As the chick breathed, the oxygen inside the egg was replaced by the chick's carbon dioxide. The gas twitched her muscles. The head wobbled, the body stiffened. A fragment of shell lifted, and fresh air rushed in. The chick lay still. Hours passed. The other two chicks went through the same ordered sequence of hatching. Each step was vital to their safe entrance into the world.

After struggling another day, the first chick cut a larger hole and thrust her beak and egg tooth into the air. She breathed freely.

She rested, letting her lungs became fully functional.

While she was quiet, Frightful stepped off the eggs and 426 stood over them.

On day thirty-one, the chicks' heads were circling inside their shells, cutting through them.

The sandblasters screamed below; work platforms clanged in the wind. Frightful and 426 heard nothing. They were hatching the chicks.

The little female cut through two-thirds of the shell top, then pushed the cap with her shoulders. It popped open. She stuck her head out.

A cherry picker rolled out onto the bridge and lifted Dan Martin to the top of the bow. He sanded the rust by hand, checking to make sure he wasn't disturbing the peregrines. Frightful was on the nest, her feathers draped around the hatching chicks.

Once her head was out, the first chick, a wet little female, easily kicked herself free of the shell.

A peregrine falcon was born. She was Oksi, the wide-eyed.

Frightful let her feathers fall over Oksi while the little bird rested from her great struggle. 426 perched quietly by.

In about an hour the chick was dry and fuzzy white. Her wings were stubs, her eyes closed. Her beak and feet were enormous. She wobbled.

Finally the workers quit for the day. The other two chicks hatched to the peaceful sound of wind playing on the webs of the Delhi Bridge.

That second day of June was cold. Snow clouds hung over the river and valley. The mountain laurel tightened their leaves, and the apple blossoms froze.

Frightful did not feel the grip of the arctic cold. Her

chicks were under her breast feathers, nestled against her brood patch; her wings were around them like insulating blankets.

Sam was back in his lean-to. He put down his binoculars.

"Good girl," he said.

Below him in the Victorian house, the falcon fan club was peering through the spotting scope in Molly's room.

"Three babies," Molly said. Her eyes twinkled. "I saw them when the mom stood up."

"Lemme see," said Maria, and adjusted the focus on the scope. "Aw, phooey, she's sitting on them."

"Three babies!" said Hughie. "They can't paint the bridge now."

"Wanna bet?" asked José.

"No," Hughie answered, "I don't."

"Let's write the governor again," Maria said. "We'll tell him about the babies. He loves babies. He said so."

"Tell him we'll name them after his kids if he stops the work," said Molly. "That might do it."

"Wanna bet?" asked José.

Over the wind that was piping among the webs of the bridge, Frightful heard Sam's whistle. It came from the mountainside. She turned her head his way but did not answer. The three chicks were nestled under her. She was part of them. She moved as they moved. She slept when they slept. For the first time, Frightful felt the all-consuming oneness of motherhood.

The bridge was quiet. 426 flew in and perched near Frightful.

The three eyases did not eat.

The kids in Molly's room worried. Sam worried.

Frightful did nothing about it. She bellied up to the little peregrines and looked admiringly at each individual.

Oksi, the falcon and the first hatched, was bigger than the two tiercels. Her eyes were large and penetrating.

"Pseee," Oksi called late in the afternoon. 426 pulled off a tiny bite of meat and fed her. The chick was still living on egg-sac food and did not need the morsel of liver, but it started her digestive tract working.

"Kak, kak, kak, kak, kak." This call came from Screamer. Frightful fed him a bite.

Before dusk, Blue Bill, a spunky tiercel with an unusually dark beak, called to his parents, and a snip of liver started his system working.

Sunday the bridge was quiet. Sam planted potatoes for Mrs. Strawberry and went back to his home in the hemlock tree.

Frightful mothered her chicks. The fumes from tourist traffic rose as the sun warmed the roads. Frightful blinked as it burned her eyes, but she did not leave.

Around noon, 426 circled over the courthouse park,

eyes on all movements. A child wheeled his tricycle down the sidewalk, sending the pigeons into the sunlight like water-splash. 426 swooped, caught one on the wing, and brought it back to the aerie. He gave bites to Frightful, who, ever so precisely, placed the bites into the open mouths of the eyases.

On Monday morning, Joe Cassini and Dan Martin arrived at the bridge early.

"The Transportation Department still says I must go ahead with the painting," Joe said to Dan. "So the plan is this: First we'll paint all the webs but number five. Then we'll do the big horizontal girder and the bow. By the time we get that far, the babies'll be about ten days old."

"Then what do we do? They can't fly then, can they?"

"No, not according to Leon Longbridge," Joe Cassini said, looking up at the aerie. "But he did say that when they were ten days old and pretty well feathered, he could move them to the box in the sycamore tree. Said their parents will feed them for sure."

"Maybe this mother won't do that," said Dan Martin. "She's a funny bird. She's not too motherly when she's not on her aerie. I've seen her flying off toward that mountain upriver and staying a long time."

"Dan," Joe Cassini said, "you get up there and paint the webs, but don't scare them away. I've got a soft spot for that family." Joe Cassini looked at the top of the bow. "I'll give you a cherry picker if you need one."

"I don't," Dan said, and walked along the bridge to study the complex webbing.

A dark-green pickup truck pulled up to the roadblock on the town side of the bridge, and a lean man in a green uniform got out. He surveyed the webs and bow of the bridge, then walked over to Joe and Dan.

"Good morning," he said. "I'm Flip Pearson from the U.S. Fish and Wildlife Service."

They shook hands.

"I understand you have a peregrine falcon nesting on this bridge," Flip Pearson said.

"Yeah," Joe Cassini answered. "A pair."

"I've been sent by Washington to move the eyases to another site." A second man got out of the pickup and joined him. "This is Dr. Werner, our peregrine expert."

"Pleased to meet you," Joe Cassini said. The doctor nodded but did not acknowledge the greeting. His dark hair almost covered thick black eyebrows that shadowed a thin face. He did not even speak.

"It's important to save those birds," Flip said.

"It sure is," said Joe Cassini. "There's an awful lot of opinion around here to do just that."

"Think you can move them?" Dan Martin asked. "The state tried once. But it didn't work."

"That's what I understand," said Flip Pearson. "But they moved eggs, not eyases." Dr. Werner glanced up at the bridge.

"Eyases are a whole different ball game," Flip Pearson went on. "Once the chicks are hatched, the parents will take care of them wherever you move them."

"Are you going to put them in the sycamore tree?" asked Joe Cassini.

"No," Flip answered. "That's too low. No peregrine would come that low and that close to the traffic."

"Is that so?" said Joe Cassini. "I guess the conservation officer didn't think of that."

"That's why the falcons didn't come back to the eggs," Flip said. "Too low."

"Well," said Joe Cassini, "what can we do to help you?"

"The faster we move, the better," said Flip Pearson. "Could you bring the cherry picker up to the nest?"

"Dan," said Joe Cassini, "you can operate the cherry picker, can't you?"

"Yeah," he said. "But won't it freak them out?"

"The quicker we take them, the quicker the birds will adjust," said Flip. Dr. Werner nodded a strong affirmative.

"There'll be some panic," Flip said. "But when we relocate the eyases, the parents will calm down."

"You sure?"

"Yes, I am."

Dan Martin started the cherry picker and drove it under

the aerie. He lowered the bucket; Flip got in and was hoisted to the nest.

Molly was watching from her bedroom window. She focused the spotting scope on the door of the green pickup. "U.S. Fish and Wildlife Service," she read, and got on the phone.

"Hughie," she said. "Call the kids and tell them to come down to the bridge right away. The U.S. Fish and Wildlife Service is finally doing something about the peregrines."

"What?"

"Moving them, I think." She hung up.

Frightful did not see the cherry picker until Flip's head and arm came up over the horizontal girder. She took off in panic. 426 followed her. They climbed above the bridge and swooped down on the man. Frightful struck his head as he reached into the scrape and grabbed the eyases.

"Lower away," Flip yelled when he had the little falcons in a canvas pack. Dan Martin brought the cherry picker back to the ground. Flip climbed out and hurried toward the pickup truck with the pack.

"Let's see the babies," Molly called from the bridge barricades. Hughie was standing beside her with his mouth wide open. Maria arrived, then José. They pushed toward Flip.

"Can we see the babies?" José asked excitedly. Flip held the bag against his chest and shoved the kids back. Joe Cassini stepped up to him.

"Let them take one peek," he said. "These are the kids

that have been holding parades and writing letters to save the peregrines."

Flip Pearson looked at the falcon expert. He nodded but still said nothing.

"Okay," said Flip. "Step close, and I'll let you see."

He opened the bag. Molly looked in.

"There're only two," she said.

"That's all there were—two."

"I saw three," insisted Molly.

"Mortality is high during the first few days of a bird's life," said Flip. "There were only two."

Screamer let out a terrible cry, and Flip closed the bag.

"Okay, kids, back off," Flip said angrily. "We've got to get these birds to their new home before they die, too." He followed Dr. Werner to the pickup. Molly was close behind.

"Where are you taking them?" she asked.

"I can't tell you," Flip said. "Against regulations. These birds are protected by federal law." Dr. Werner started the motor.

The truck pulled away and sped down Elm Street, turned right at the T, and disappeared behind the bank and the café.

"Where's Leon Longbridge?" Hughie asked suddenly.

"Didn't you call him?" Molly asked.

"I thought he would know. The Feds must have told him they were coming."

The kids looked at each other. Their eyes widened.

"You see Leon Longbridge?" José asked Joe Cassini.

"Not this morning," he said.

"He'll sure be glad to know someone finally moved those birds," said Dan Martin.

"Wanna bet?" said José as he started running for Leon Longbridge's office.

The school bell rang.

"Cree, cree, cree, kak, kak, kak."

High above the Delhi Bridge, Frightful screamed and spiraled, her pointed wings cutting frantic patterns in the sky.

IN WHICH

Sam Takes Charge

Sam was at his lean-to, his elbows propped on his knees, his binocs pinned on the green pickup. He had watched the two U.S. Fish and Wildlife Service men rescue the peregrine eyases of the Delhi Bridge. He was grateful to them. The bridge painting was becoming intolerable.

Sam studied them closely. The dark-haired man seemed familiar, but he didn't know any Fish and Wildlife Service people. He turned his glasses on Frightful. She zoomed out of nowhere and landed on the scrape.

Why wasn't she following the Feds and her eyases? She was not even looking in their direction. And then he saw why. An eyas appeared and nestled into her warm breast feathers.

"What the heck!" Sam said aloud. "She's feeding!"

He put down his glasses and whistled his "come here" notes to Frightful.

Frightful turned her head but did not answer. She was mothering Oksi and calling a worried "kak, kak" to 426. He came down from a height where no human eye could see him, landed on the girder, and took off again. The man in the cherry picker had so terrified him, he could not force himself to sit on the bridge. He caught a wind and was sped up the mountain. He came to rest on a large maple near Sam's lean-to and flattened his feathers to his body. His eye pupils were pinpoints of fear.

"Kak, kak, kak." 426 yelled the distress cry over and over.

Sam lowered his glasses to the bridge span. The men on the paint crew were swinging the work platforms under the fifth web, getting ready to paint the seemingly empty aerie. Down on Elm Street, Molly, José, and Leon Longbridge came on the run.

They joined Joe Cassini and Dan Martin at the cherry picker.

"Good news," Joe said. "The Feds moved the little birds."

"No, they didn't," Leon said. "They stole them. Those men were not from the U.S. Fish and Wildlife Service. I checked on them when Hughie called me. And they weren't from the state, either."

"Who were they, then?"

"Poachers—a special kind of poacher," said Leon. "They'll raise the eyases and sell them for tens of thousands of dollars."

"Did you get their license plate number?" Molly asked Joe hopefully.

"No," he answered. "Never occurred to me they weren't legit. But they should be easy to find. They were in an old green Chevy pickup with an official insignia on the door."

"What'll we do?" José asked, tugging Leon Longbridge's sleeve.

"I've already called the police," he said. "Also Jon Wood. He suspects some poachers are hiding out in a cabin on White Man Mountain. Maybe we should begin there."

"Can we come?" Molly asked, clapping her hands.

"No," Leon said forcefully. "Those guys are dangerous. Now, run along to school. You're late."

When Leon went back to his office, Joe Cassini and Dan Martin looked up at the intricately webbed bridge that had been a home for the peregrines. Its crisscrossed grid was a huge silver tapestry in the gray spring light.

"Well, Dan," Joe said, "the falcons are gone. We'll sandblast the aerie. Nothing to stop us from painting now."

"Except that thunderstorm hanging over the mountain," Dan Martin answered. "I'm going to sit this one out. I don't want to be caught in a thunderstorm on an iron bridge." He closed his paint bucket and returned it to the supply truck.

Joe Cassini was checking the sanding job on the bridge railing when the first peal of thunder rumbled. He called the men down from the work platforms and sent them to the safety of their cars. In his own car he took out a thermos of coffee, drank several gulps, then leaned back and closed his eyes.

"How was I to know wildlife officials from poachers?"

he asked himself. "Well, I hope they get caught. I got real fond of those birds." Lightning flashed like fireworks.

Oksi pressed up against Frightful and crawled deeper into her feathers. Both sat still and waited. The falling air pressure foretold a severe storm.

Sam felt the warning, too, but he planned to take advantage of it. He walked down the mountainside to the road and sat under a large rhododendron bush. The clouds rolled over Delhi in blue-black boils, their bottoms illuminated by white flashes. A few large raindrops splattered down onto the rhododendron leaves, then many. A fork of lightning opened a cloud. It closed with a thunderous boom. Water spilled down in sheets.

When he could no longer see Joe Cassini's car for the rain, Sam crawled out from under the bush and ran to the bowed arch. Barefoot, using his hands and feet, he went up it. The rain poured off his hair and down his face. Lightning danced over the bridge and town. The thunder became a continuous boom. When he got to where the bow met the fifth vertical web, Sam whistled three notes.

There was no response.

Dropping to the horizontal girder, he flattened out on his belly.

"Frightful?" he whispered. "Are you there?" The rain deluged, flooding the girder and running into the aerie.

"Creee, creee, creee, car-reet."

"Hey, Frightful," he said. "I'm going to take the little falcon to our home. Follow me." He slipped his hand under her. She did not move.

"Lift up. Pssst, psst. I love you. It's all right."

Sam wormed forward until his hand closed over a small, warm body. Frightful *kakak*-ed and flew into the rain.

He put Oksi inside his shirt against his chest, then tied a leather thong around his waist so that she wouldn't fall out. He backed down the bow.

A jagged white lightning bolt hit the steeple of the church near the courthouse. A boom of thunder as loud as a cannonade shook the bridge.

"Too close," said Sam. "Let's get off this thing."

He jumped to the ground, glancing back to see if anyone had noticed him. Not much chance. The rain was falling so hard that he could barely see the cherry picker in the middle of the span. Picking up his moccasins, he crossed the road and went up the mountain.

He did not stop at his bivouac. Moving quickly, he took a deer trail to the long path that led up the one mountain to the one tree. He hurried. Little falcons needed constant food.

From time to time he glanced up through the rain, hoping to see Frightful above them. The deluge was too heavy to see anything beyond gray streaks of water.

"She'll know where I'm going," he said, and ran on up the trail.

When he stepped into the ancient hemlock, Oksi was still warm and dry inside his shirt. He put her on the floor. Oksi sat back on her heels and screamed without letup while he changed into the new suit he had made from the hide of a road-killed deer. He lit a fire and sat on his bed. The eyas screamed on.

"Your mom," he said softly, "will find you as soon as the storm stops. This is her first home."

Oksi cried louder, opening her beak to be fed.

Outside, the rain kept falling.

"Kak, kak, kak"—the peregrine worry call.

Sam grinned and poked his head out the deerskin door, expecting to see Frightful. He saw only rain bending the branches of the hemlocks and running in rivulets down their trunks.

"Where are you, Frightful?" he called. "Your eyas is very hungry. I don't want to feed her. She will imprint on me and think she's a person. Then she will never mate with her kind."

"Kak, kak, kak."

The frightened peregrine falcon called again. "Let it be Frightful," Sam said, squinting up through the big hemlock limbs at an erect, broad-shouldered bird near the top.

He whistled. The bird shook off the rain.

"Too small to be Frightful," Sam mused. "It's her mate. But he's not much use. He won't feed the eyas at this stage of the game. She's too old. We've got to find Frightful." The eyas screamed so hard that Sam's ears rang. He found Frightful's old hood and deftly put it over Oksi's head. She immediately stopped screaming.

Dashing out through the rain, Sam entered the mill house and picked up a box he had made with boards Bando had cut for his furniture and discarded. The box had five sides. If the box that Leon Longbridge had used was a model, Sam's needed one more thing. He picked up a slat of wood about three inches wide and bored holes in it. Next he bored holes at the edge of the box opening. With his penknife he whittled sticks to make pegs and fastened the board to the box with them. The board was just high enough to prevent the eyas from falling out. He had a home for Frightful and her baby.

When he was done, the rain had stopped, and the thunder rumbled down the valley. Sam returned to the little falcon and took off her hood. She screamed for food. Hoping she was hungry enough to eat on her own, Sam took a deer mouse out of the pocket of the rain-drenched suit.

"I trapped this at the lean-to," he said to Oksi. "A guy never knows when he'll need a mouse in this life." Oksi fluttered her fuzzy white wings and screamed louder. She was frantic and close to the first stage of starvation.

"You've got to eat this by yourself," Sam said, and threw the mouse on the ground. She did not even look at it, just up at him, and screamed continually.

Sam put the hood back on her head and went outside. He strapped the nest box to his back and, gripping the lowest limb of the hemlock, swung hand over hand to the tree trunk.

"Kak, kak, kak."

Sam looked up. 426 flew out of the hemlock, circled, and disappeared.

"That *is* Frightful's mate," he said. "I recognize the broad band on the tip of his tail."

He whistled for Frightful, but she did not appear, and he climbed on up, limb by limb.

"Where is she?" he asked himself. "She should have been right above me—even in the rain. Did I put too much faith in our friendship? I thought she knew I was taking her eyas to our tree. I was so sure she would follow me.

"I was wrong."

Sam stopped where two limbs made a secure brace for the box and tied it to the trunk and both limbs. He tested it several times for stability, then climbed down.

"If this doesn't work," he said aloud, "I'll have to feed the little eyas. That will change her whole life.

"I also might be jailed for harboring an endangered species."

I N W H I C H
Sam Battles Bird Instincts

Frightful had completely panicked when Sam reached under her in the thunderous storm. She flew into the drenching rain and gained altitude, ready to strike him with all the force of her speeding body.

A powerful gust of wind caught her wings and swept her upriver. Its downdraft pulled her toward the water. She fought wind and rain to get back to the bridge, but the storm was the master. She gave up and dropped into a calm eddy of air behind a bank of willows.

"Creee, creee, creee," she called from a dead stub. Lightning burned streaks in the sky, and thunder cannonaded.

"Creee," she called once more, then pulled her head down between her shoulders and let the rain run off her body.

Through the storm she listened for 426. She had last seen him swooping down on the man in the cherry picker.

"Creee."

There was no answer from 426.

She waited in the willow tree until her fear subsided. It was short-lived. In moments she was quietly listening to the rain slap the leaves around her.

After a long time, the deluge stopped.

In less than two seconds, Frightful was back on the horizontal girder of the bridge. She walked to the wet scrape, turning under her talons so as not to injure the young.

"Creee," she called. No eyas answered, nor did 426.

At recess Molly and José came splashing through big puddles to the bridge. They stood before it, looking up at the webs and the graceful bow.

"The bridge has changed," Molly said. "It's dead."

"Yeah," said José. "No peregrines. Not even a coat of red paint can make it fun again."

The two walked along the bank and watched frogs jump into the river until the bell rang at the end of recess. They started back. Leon Longbridge pulled up beside them.

"Listen to this," he said, waving a paper. "It's from the governor."

"Read it. Read it, please," said José.

"It's addressed to me and the students of Delhi Middle School." He began:

Thank you for your many well-written letters concerning the peregrines of Delhi Bridge.

I am pleased to inform you that I share your concern. Work will stop on the bridge on Route 28 until the young peregrine falcons are fledged.

Although the bridge repair is urgent, our endangered

*species, once gone, cannot be brought back. Therefore I
have told the head of the Transportation Department of the
State of New York to work on Bridge 92 at Gilboa until the
little family is on wing.*

*My administration actively protects the environment of
New York State, and I am happy you are in favor of this policy.*
Sincerely,
Governor George Marki

"Too late," Molly whispered, tears in her eyes.

"For lack of understanding," Leon Longbridge said,
"we've lost three beautiful eyases."

"Can I read the letter?" Molly asked.

"I've made you a copy," Leon said, handing her a paper.
"And one for you, José."

After rereading the letter three times, José folded it and
put it in his pocket.

"We've got to catch the poachers," he said. "We've got
to get the babies back." He turned hopelessly to Leon
Longbridge. "How can we do that?"

"The state troopers are looking for them right now,"
Leon said, "and the Department of Motor Vehicles is
checking the ownership of all the Chevy pickups. So far
nothing."

Molly put the letter in her book and, without another
word, walked back to school. José walked silently behind
her.

Frightful stared into her empty scrape.

Restless and upset, she flew to the park, caught a pigeon, and carried it to the cupola of the courthouse. She ate and watched for 426.

When she was comfortably full, she carried the remains back to the scrape and tore off an eyas bite. There were no open beaks to fill. She peered at the girder, waiting for the little falcons to thrust up their heads. They did not. She swallowed the food.

Frightful did not leave the aerie. Her mothering instincts were strong. She still felt the presence of her chicks. But as the hours passed and her eyases did not appear, the feeling began to fade. Without her young to inspire her, it would not take many days for the nurturing instinct to die.

In the early afternoon, Frightful left the bridge and flew over the town, the river, the mountains, in wider and wider circles.

Eventually she flew over 426, perched on the one hemlock on the one mountain. In seconds she was beside him.

A movement below caught her eye. She tipped her head. Sam had stepped out of the tree.

"Creee, creee, creee, car-reet," she called.

"Frightful!" he cried joyfully. "Where are you? I hear you." He whistled and stepped back.

"Oh, Frightful," he said when he saw her. "I have your little eyas. She's right here. Follow me."

Sam put Oksi into his soft backpack, shouldered it, and

started climbing. 426 cried out the peregrine alarm and
sped off. Frightful stayed.

When Sam reached the nest box, she was only ten feet
above him. He held up the eyas.

"Here she is. You must feed her. She's hungry."

He placed the downy chick in the box and hurriedly
climbed to the ground.

Frightful watched him.

Sam watched her.

There were no hunger cries from Oksi. She was too per-
plexed by the box. She sat still, waiting for her mother.
Oksi could not see Frightful from inside the enclosure, and
Frightful could not see Oksi from where she was sitting.
She must hear the eyas call to locate her.

Sam paced and watched from below. The little bird
needed food and needed it right away. A few hours without
eating at this time of Oksi's life would put hunger streaks in
her feathers. Weakened, they would break when she was
old enough to fly.

Sam got his falconer's lure from the hemlock house. It
was a chunk of deer hide with pheasant feathers tied to it.
He spun it around his head on a long line. In action, the
lure looked like a bird—food. Frightful had once been so
well trained, she came to the lure even when she was not
hungry, but that was long ago. She cocked her head and
looked with interest at the whirling lure. Sam whistled.

She sat. Finally Sam tied the mouse to it and swung it again.

Frightful saw the mouse. She dropped swiftly, hit it, and went with it to the ground. Sam picked her up.

"Frightful, gal," he said, blowing out his breath in relief, "you've got a job to do. The eyas is in that box in the tree. She's in trouble. She needs you."

Frightful did not understand the words, but she did understand Sam's worried mood. She sat on his hand and looked at him.

"I'm going to climb the tree with you," he said. "No, you'll fly if I do that. I'd better jess you first."

Sam carried her into the hemlock tree.

"Creee," she called, recognizing the cozy interior of the one tree on the one mountain. She roused and sat contentedly.

Sam cut two thin pieces of deer hide, made three holes in each, and, tucking ends inside holes, he fastened jesses to her legs with the falconer's knot, the knot that never binds.

Frightful felt the jesses go taut as Sam gripped them between his thumb and forefinger. It was a familiar feeling. She wiped her beak on his fist and sat erect. He walked outside.

"No one had better see us now," he said with a chuckle. "I'd be hauled off to jail for practicing falconry without a license." Frightful fluffed. Sam started climbing.

His maneuvers around limbs were jerky, and Frightful thrust out her wings to keep her balance. Twice she tried to fly.

They finally reached the box. Sam placed her in it.

"Pseee," called Oksi.

Frightful heard the feeble cry of her chick. In her eagerness to reach her, she struck the box hard with her wings. The hollow sound was terrifying. She took off.

"Oh, no," Sam gasped. "You're wearing jesses. I'm in real trouble if anyone sees you." Then he added, "But I don't care. You know where the eyas is. You'll come back and feed her."

Frightful screamed as she flew around the mountaintop in wider and wider circles. She calmed down, remembered the hunger cry of her eyas, and dove gracefully toward the tree.

Suddenly, a red-tailed hawk grabbed Frightful's jesses, mistaking them for food. He pulled her downward, then let go before they both fell into the trees.

Catching herself on her acrobatic wings, Frightful skimmed up through and over the trees. She flew down the mountain like a hurtled rock and alighted on the Delhi Bridge. Panting, she gazed at the river until she was calm.

The painters were back at work.

A car screeched to a stop, and the driver pinned his binoculars on Frightful.

"I'll be darned," said Perry Knowlton, a falconer. He picked up his car phone and called his friend Jon Wood.

"Lose a peregrine?" he asked.

"No; why, you see one?"

"Yeah, and she's wearing jesses," Perry said.

"Where are you?"

"I'm at the Delhi Bridge. There's a jessed falcon on the bow. What do you make of that?"

"There was a pair of wild falcons nesting there," said Jon, "but they didn't have jesses. Call Leon Longbridge; he might have heard about a lost falcon. I can't come help you. I've a week of school shows coming up."

"I'll try to follow her," Perry said, and hung up.

Frightful dove into a flock of pigeons wheeling out over the river, snatched one in the air, and flew on.

Perry watched her as he drove along the riverside highway. When she flew up-mountain he parked, jumped from his car, and kept her in sight until she disappeared. Then he picked up the car phone and dialed Leon Longbridge. His answering machine went on.

"This is Perry, Leon," he said into the machine. "There's a jessed peregrine flying around here. Jon Wood doesn't know anything about her. She's just gone up the river toward Treadwell. I'll drive along that road and ask the residents if they know anyone who has a falcon around here." He thought a moment, and went on, "Would you call your boss in Albany and inquire about licensed falconers in this area? I don't know of any except Jon Wood and me; but there may be others."

Frightful was over Sam's mountain, hovering above the one tree, searching for her eyas. The roof of the box prevented her from seeing inside. She flew to a large oak. This was a familiar tree. On its broad limbs sat the wigwam Sam had made for Alice. Alice was not at home.

Frightful bobbed her head and twisted it as she stared at the box in the hemlock. Oksi was there. As much as she disliked flying through forest limbs, she must. Hopping from oak to maple to hickory to tulip tree, the pigeon still in her talons, she made her way to the top of the ancient hemlock.

"Kak, kak, kak, kak." Frightful cried the alarm call of the peregrine and dove at a monsterlike creature in the tree. She did not scare it. It moved closer to Oksi.

The bulky thing had a tanned chicken—feathers, head, comb, and all—for a head. A burlap bag hung down from it. The head moved into the box. In its beak was food. Oksi snatched it and ate. The monster withdrew and returned with more food. Oksi gulped.

The ogre disappeared, and Oksi came to the edge of the box. She peered down at this strange mother. The head wiggled as hands stuck food into the chicken beak. Then the monster mother climbed back to her. Oksi ate. She ate until her crop stuck out and she could eat no more. The monster mother went down the tree to the ground.

Sam Gribley took off the burlap bag on which he had affixed Alice's whole tanned chicken skin. He looked for Frightful.

"I scared her badly," he said aloud, "but at least her eyas ate. She didn't see my face, so she won't imprint on me." Then he thought about what he had done and chuckled. He spoke aloud.

"You had better come back and feed her, Frightful," he said, "or she'll be imprinted on a monster chicken."

Sam drove a stick into the ground and drew a line along its shadow. The shadow would move away from the line as the sun moved. He could tell by the distance it traveled how much time had passed. At this time of year, it would move three and one-half inches each hour.

"The little eyas is good for maybe three hours," he said to himself. "If Frightful doesn't come by then, I'll have to be a chicken monster again." He grinned and went inside his tree to write in his journal.

"I think I gave Frightful an awful scare," he wrote.

The hours passed. The stick shadow moved ten-and-a-half inches—three hours. Frightful sat motionless on a tree stub above the West Branch of the Delaware. She was still afraid but, at the same time, pulled to her chick in the one tree.

The sun shone on her blue-gray shoulders and gleamed in her large eyes. Her feet gripped the dead limb more and more tightly. She could not relax.

Hunger finally forced her to move. She flew up the river valley, spotted a rat moving along the side of a farm silo, and took it. She carried it to the courthouse cupola.

Tenderly she plucked a bite and held it in her beak, waiting for an eyas to take it. None did. She swallowed it.

Suddenly Frightful's need to return to her eyas overwhelmed her fears. She spread her long, tapered wings and flew toward Oksi, rat in her talons. A soft wind carried her swiftly up the mountainside. She circled the one hemlock. No monster with a chicken head hung in the branch. Frightful landed on the tree.

The box and the eyas were gone.

"Creee, creee, creee, car-reet," she cried.

"Not the tree," Sam called from below. "The eyas is on the roof of the mill house. I put her out in the open where a peregrine's aerie should be."

Frightful saw Oksi.

She sped down, food in her talons, and landed on the floor of the box.

Oksi screamed.

Sam watched, his fists clenched, his body tense.

Frightful tore off a morsel and fed Oksi.

"Phew!" Sam let out a long, long breath.

IN WHICH
A Pal Finds a Pal

Oksi was six days old on that eventful day. She was a ball of white fuzz with huge shining eyes rimmed with saffron. Her beak was pale blue. She had two needs: food and Frightful's warm brood patch, and now, at last, she had both. She crawled into her mother's breast feathers and sat quietly.

Sam closed down the waterwheel early and carried wood to his stone oven to make a fire. The oven sat a few yards away from his table and the four tree-stump chairs. All were in the umbra of the magnificent hemlock. When the fire was lit, he wrapped cattail tubers and trout in two large may-apple leaves and placed them in the oven. Then he rested his elbow on the table and scratched his head.

The dark-haired man came back to mind. Sam jumped to his feet.

"Skri! Bate!" he said out loud. He thought a moment. "It's eyas time. The poachers are at work for that Arabian agent again." Sam remembered how Sean Conklin and he had caught Skri leaving a cave at Beaver Corners last June. With him was the man called Bate and his friend.

"That's it; Skri and Bate took the eyases." He sat down again. "But where are they?"

While his supper cooked, his mind ran over all the possible answers to his question.

"Bate won't be at his home in Altamont—too risky. They all know him." He thought harder. "Seems he goes incognito," he recalled. "He told me he was Leon Longbridge, and he told Joe Cassini he was a government official. He's got to be someplace where he can act like somebody else and get away with it. Where's that?"

The sun went down, and the troublesome day was over. Alice came up the twilit trail with a basket of sweet wild strawberries from Mrs. Strawberry's field. She sat down on a log stump at the table and decapped one.

"I have a dog," she said, handing Sam the strawberry.

"A dog?" said Sam, popping it into his mouth, then poking a stick into the trout to test its doneness. "I thought you were a pig girl."

"Pigs are best," said Alice, "but this dog is special."

"Where did you get him?"

"Remember Hanni?"

Sam blushed and smiled.

"Of course I remember Hanni. What about Hanni?"

"Well, she and Hendrik found this dog over near the Helderberg Escarpment and took him home. He was so terrified of people he chewed his leash and got away. Last week when Hanni was visiting the John Burroughs lodge, she found him again."

"What was he doing at the John Burroughs lodge?"

"Denning under it and living off the land, like he does."

"Smart dog." Sam smiled. "I like his spirit."

"Except there were two Park Service rangers there who were trying to shoot him for catching game. That's dumb."

"Maybe. What happened?"

"Hanni told them the dog was hers and took him home again."

"She and Hendrik brought him to me. Hanni thought I could bring the love of people to him, like I did to Crystal, my pig." Alice smiled. "The dog's adorable—a yellow cur with long ears; big, sad eyes—and the best rabbit chaser I've ever seen."

"What's his name?"

"Hendrik and Hanni named him General, but their aunt and uncle said the people they bought the farm from called him Mole. He lived in a culvert. I like the name Mole."

"So do I. And where is Mole?"

"Down at the farm with Mrs. Strawberry. I'm going back. I just want to get some rawhide from you to make him a special collar. I want to braid it into a tough band so he can't get loose."

"Sure he won't eat it?"

"He can't reach it, silly," Alice said.

"Alice," Sam said, taking his supper out of the oven, "did you say Hanni talked to two rangers at the John Burroughs house?"

"Yes; you know, the Park Service owns it."

"But the Park Service doesn't own it. It is owned by descendants of the John Burroughs family. There're no rangers on duty there. Bando and I camped there when we were looking for you last spring."

"Well, whatever—two men were going to shoot him."

Sam shared his meal with Alice. The trout was tender, but the cattail tubers were tough. When they had finished their meal with the delicious strawberries, Sam got deer hide from the mill house and cut off long strips for Alice.

"Thanks," Alice said, and put them into her pocket. "I'm off now, to bring love to Mole."

Sam was out of bed early the next morning. Barefoot and lacing up his deerskin shirt as he stepped outside, he looked over the pond into Frightful's nest box. He had placed it so that the opening faced him. Frightful was far back in the corner, mothering. Although all seemed well, it was not. There was no tiercel. Sam would have to bring food to Frightful until 426 came back. The eyas was still too young for Frightful to leave her and hunt.

While Sam cooked cornmeal mush for breakfast, Frightful came to the front of the box and scanned the skies, looking for 426. Oksi was screaming to be fed. The air was chilly.

She called for her mate. He did not answer.

Around noon, when the air had warmed, Frightful gave the little eyas the last bites of the rat. Then she sat down and brooded her.

Sam whistled that he had food for her, but she did not fly to him. Oksi was shivering. She needed her mother's warmth.

Several hours later, Frightful stood up and walked to the edge of the box. She called for a new mate. She called over and over again.

Then down from the clouds, over the feathery tips of the hemlocks, came Chup. He circled the mill house and dropped onto its stovepipe.

"Chup, chup," he called, and flew to the box. 426 was dead. He would not have permitted another male in his territory had he been alive.

"Creee," she called.

Chup also was single. His mate had not returned to their aerie one morning, and he was forced to be mother and hunter to three eyases again. This time he had been unable to call in a mate, and his chicks had not survived.

The day they succumbed to starvation, he flew down the Schoharie gorge and up over the mountains of Delhi. He cried in distress. Gliding over Peaks Brook, he heard Frightful calling for a new mate. He folded his wings and dropped down onto the mill-house roof. He jumped up to the nest box and bowed to her. Frightful looked at her mate of last spring as if it were perfectly natural for him to be there.

Chup looked at Oksi and without even a signal from Frightful, walked to Oksi and dropped his feathers over her. Frightful flew off to hunt. She sped to the abandoned meadow, now pale green with raspberry and young hawthorn leaves. She hovered, watching for game.

A rabbit jumped up and darted away. Frightful stooped and did not miss.

She was on the ground with it when she heard a dog woof. She covered the food with her wings, then looked around. Peering through the bushes at her was Mole, his head twisting in curiosity. He recognized Frightful. Frightful recognized him. He came toward her. He wanted some rabbit.

This was no time to share. Frightful clutched the food in her talons and beak, and with deep wing beats was airborne. She gained altitude, maneuvered, and steered through the trees to the mill house. She and the rabbit landed with a thud in the box.

Only Oksi's tail feathers showed beneath Chup. He stood up and without making a sound, flew to the top of the hemlock. Frightful fed the eyas.

Sam was dipping a water bucket into the millpond when he saw Chup leave the nest box.

"Hey, that's Frightful's mate!" he exclaimed. "Great—I'm relieved of my tiercel duties, and just in time."

He hurried to the root cellar and packed his rucksack with enough nuts, venison jerky, and big potatolike Jerusalem artichoke roots to feed himself for three or four days.

He was adding dried apples when he heard a suspicious noise, and moved a sack of dry corn.

"Jessie Coon James," Sam exclaimed. "Where have you been all these months?" He rolled his tongue, imitating a raccoon purr, and held out his hand. His old friend waddled up to him, ears down in deference.

"Got a family?" Sam asked. "Must not, or you'd have them with you and I would be foodless."

Jessie Coon James took an ear of corn in both forepaws and chewed.

"Give me that corn, you bandit," he said and, laughing happily to see his old friend again, picked her up and hugged her. Jessie grabbed the corn tighter.

"Oh, all right," he said. "You can have one ear." Jessie took it in her teeth and dropped to the floor. Sam watched her. Jessie departed through a tunnel she had dug under the door.

"Aha," he said. "I'd better fix that before I go, or I won't have any food when I get home." Then he added, "Speaking of fixing things, I'd better remember to remove Frightful's jesses. I don't want anyone to come by here and see her with those on. They'll fine me for harboring an endangered species."

An hour later, when the hole was mended and Frightful's jesses removed, Molly and José were walking across the Delhi Bridge. Molly looked up at the empty nest site.

"José," she said, "we've got to find the baby falcons."

"How?" he asked helplessly. "Leon Longbridge has the police looking all over three counties, and they can't find them. How can we?"

"By remembering things." She rubbed her forehead. "Last spring the newspaper said the sheriff arrested some falcon poachers in a cave at Beaver Corners. I'll bet they are the ones who stole the eyases, and I'll bet they're right there now."

"And just how do we get there?"

"We tell Leon Longbridge. He'll take us."

"He might," said José, then beamed. "I hope so. I love caves."

Leon Longbridge, they learned, had already checked the cave and found nothing. Molly and José went back to the bridge to think some more.

At that moment Sam was walking across his mountain meadow when he heard the clinking of a chain. He scanned the field and forest edge. A hawthorn bush trembled. He stole up on it.

"Well, who are you?" he said to a dog, whose broken chain was wrapped twice around the hawthorn. The dog wore a braided leather collar.

"You're Mole," Sam answered himself. "That's who you are." Mole wagged his tail.

"You should be named Houdini. You get out of every leash, collar, and barn you're put in." Smiling broadly, Sam got down on his knees. "And here I am getting you out of this mess." Carefully he unwound the chain, then gripped it firmly in one hand. He took Mole's chin in the other.

"You've got a lot of beagle in you," he said. "You can be a big help to me on this trip. How about coming along? You can sniff down food for the two of us—and maybe a criminal or two."

Sam started off. Mole wouldn't budge.

"Come, Mole. Come." He yanked on the leash.

Mole pulled backward, ducking down his head to slip his collar.

"I'm sorry," Sam said. "You don't want to come with me. Of course not; you don't know me. Here," he said, and held out his hand. "Let my odors tell you all about me."

Mole sniffed. Rising strong and sweet from Sam's hand were informative scents. They told Mole that Sam was a young adolescent, nonviolent, and that he liked wild foods. Mole also learned that Sam was related to Alice and that he lived in a hemlock tree. Mole finally decided he liked what he smelled and licked Sam's hand.

With that, Sam sat down and rubbed Mole's big ears. He talked to him softly, then kissed the top of his nose and told him what a good dog he was. He hugged him close.

Mole nuzzled his head under Sam's chin and whimpered softly.

"Thanks," Sam said. "I love you, too. Can we go now?" he asked.

Mole's droopy eyes sagged. Sam got up and tugged on his leash, but Mole would not move. He braced all four feet and pulled backward.

"Oh," Sam said, "I hear you. You don't like to be tied up." He took off the collar and leash and threw them into the bushes. Mole wagged his tail. Sam patted his head.

"Now, can we go?" The happy dog bounced down the mountain, sticking close to Sam's side. When the blissful pair came to the dirt road that led to Bando's house, Sam stopped.

"It would be great to have Bando along," he said, glancing in the direction of his friend's cabin. "But there's no use even asking him. He's not going to leave Zella. She's going to have a baby pretty soon."

At sundown Sam and Mole camped by an abandoned barn on the side of Mount Warren. Mole caught a feral chicken, and Sam cooked it on a small and smokeless fire.

He was an expert at making fires no one could see. When, at ten o'clock, the temperature dropped sharply, they moved into the barn and dug into a straw pile.

The next thing Sam knew, a rooster was crowing to the dawn. Sam jumped up so fast he frightened a hen. She flew off her nest, squawking and clucking, and sped out of the barn. She left behind feathers and twelve eggs. Sam helped himself to four. He boiled them hard and shared them with Mole. After washing his face in the farm spring, he and Mole resumed their trek into the dense forests of the Catskill Mountains. Later in the morning, they came to the mowed meadowlands under the power lines.

"Creee, creee, creee, car-reet."

"Desdemondia," said Sam, using Bando's respectable expletive. "That's Frightful. Only one bird calls my peregrine name."

Frightful hovered above them. "How did you find us?" he said, eyes twinkling. "Took Mole and me a day and a half to get here."

Mole dashed into the grasses and weeds. Nose to the ground, weaving in and out of young goldenrod and raspberry plants, he flushed a pheasant.

Before Sam could see whether it was a male or a female, Frightful was carrying it off toward their mountain.

"Hey!" He whistled for her to come to his hand; she flew on.

Mole barked.

In four minutes Frightful covered the air miles to her mountain. She plucked the bird on the roof of Alice's wigwam and carried the meal to the box where Chup was brooding Oksi.

Suddenly a tall, angular man stepped out of the woods. Chup gave the alarm cry and took off. Frightful sat still.

Leon Longbridge lifted his binoculars and focused them on the wooden box. "Well, I'll be," he said to himself. "There sits the falcon of Delhi Bridge. I'd know that dark, beautiful head anywhere." Then he saw the eyas.

"Wow," he said aloud. "I don't know how the two of you got here, but you're free—and that's all I'm concerned about."

He glanced around and realized he was at Sam Gribley's home. He had heard about it through young Matt, a newspaper reporter. Matt had told him that Sam had a "cool" home in a huge hemlock on a mountain. He said that he had a falcon and homemade fishhooks and fishing rods. He never told him where. Leon studied the mill house, the oven, and the stone table.

"I would sure love to live like this," he said wistfully.

Although he was curious, he did not step inside the hemlock home. He respected Sam's privacy. And so, glancing once more at Frightful, he strode down the trail, wondering how the peregrine of the Delhi Bridge and her eyas had ended up in a box on Sam's mill-house roof. He was smiling.

"Hmm," he mused. "Matt did say the kid was a falconer." He whistled a bright bird tune and thought about the bridge. "How did that kid get the eyas down from there?" he asked himself. "That must have been some act."

It took Sam and Mole until noon to reach their destination—the woods behind the John Burroughs lodge.

Sam put down his gear in a dense grove of young hemlocks.

"Stay," he said to Mole. "I'm going to climb that big tree and see what's going on. Park Service rangers at the John Burroughs Woodchuck Lodge? Humph. Some story."

Mole did not "stay." He knew perfectly well what the word meant, but he also knew where he was.

While Sam climbed the tree, Mole took his favorite fern trail to the lodge. He slipped under it, sniffing. Wood rats and a skunk had almost immediately taken over his old bedroom. He set upon the wood-rat burrow, digging downward, sending the earth flying. The rat family exited by another tunnel.

He rested a moment. The skunk must be handled differently. The den entrance was right beside his own bed at the base of the chimney. He lay down and woofed into it.

His presence should send the skunk or skunks out their back door.

Suddenly he stopped. Men were talking in the room above him; their voices vibrated the old wooden floor. His terror of people returned. Mole put his tail between his legs and slunk out from under the lodge, into the bushes. He returned to Sam's pack in the hemlock grove and lay down.

Sam jumped down from the bottom bough of the tree and hurried back to Mole.

"Good boy," he said, taking the dog's head in his hands and kissing the bridge of his muzzle. "You didn't run off." Sam rubbed Mole's big ears, then his own.

"Listen to this, Mole," he whispered. "There are two men here. I saw them through the window. I was too high to see their faces—only their feet.

"Also, there's a rabbit hutch by the toolshed." He crouched down. "Falconers raise them for falcon food.

"And down by the county road is a huge rhododendron thicket. I think I saw a green vehicle parked in the middle of it. Let's take a look.

"Come quietly, Mole." The dog rose and followed.

Sam took a circuitous route through the woods to the county road. He walked south on it, then turned onto the dirt lane that led to the lodge. The rhododendron thicket was about twenty feet back from the Burroughs's lane and about a quarter of an acre big. Sam pushed back branches and looked around. There sat the green pickup with the U.S. Fish and Wildlife Service emblem taped to its door.

"Park Service rangers don't hide their pickups," he said to Mole, and walked noiselessly around the thicket until he found where the bushes had been cut down to let the green pickup enter. He walked to the Chevy. In it were three animal-carrying cases.

"These cages don't tell me much," Sam said to the dog. "They could carry rabbits or falcons or cats or even you, Mole."

Mole began sniffing.

Sam memorized the New York license plate, then walked to the cab and looked in.

"Oh, boy," he said. "Whitewash—bird excrement. Falcons? Could be pigeons." He looked further. "A half-empty box of bullets. I don't like that, Mole."

Mole began to snuffle, sucking gobs of air over the hundreds of scent glands in his nose. Then he wagged his tail at a gray pellet on the ground.

Sam looked down.

"By golly," he said and picked up a casting from a bird of prey. He examined it carefully. It was mostly fur.

"Rabbit," he said. "The rabbits I saw are for food, and they are being fed to a falcon, an owl, a hawk, or maybe a raven." He noted the roundness of the pellet. "I say eyas—peregrine eyas."

Sam put the pellet in his pocket and walked back to the hemlock grove the way he had come. Seating himself on the ground behind the biggest tree, he cut a piece of venison jerky and gave half to Mole. Chewing on the other half, he stretched out on his back and wondered what to do next. He had to get the birds without the men seeing him. They were armed. Mole lay down beside him, the skunk on his mind.

"Looks like we've found Bate and Skri," Sam said, "and it looks like we've found the eyases."

Sam rolled over on his belly. Mole put his head on Sam's shoulder.

"We've got to be careful, old friend.

"I've got a plan," Sam said, more to himself than to Mole. "Frightful's little falcons are in the lodge. I'll get one of the rabbits and let it go in front of the lodge." Then he addressed Mole. "You'll chase the rabbit and yip so loud that the men come out to see what's going on. Then I'll go in the back door and get the eyases. I'll be up the mountain by the time Bate and his friend can get their rabbit back. You'll have to follow my trail and catch up with me.

"Got it?" Sam looked into the hound's sad, droopy eyes. "I'm not so sure you do, but I do know you'll chase anything that runs or flies."

He patted Mole's head. "Okay, this is it," he said, and headed for the rabbit hutch. He never got there.

Mole caught a whiff of the skunk and in seconds was under the lodge. He bore down on the skunk at the entrance to his den. Seeing Mole, the skunk calmly waited, then looked at him, aimed his rear end, and let loose a jet stream of musk. It burned into Mole's nose and eyes. He yiped in pain and ran around the lodge. The scent instantly seeped up through the old floor boards. It penetrated the kitchen in a yellow mist.

"Phew!" Sam recognized Bate's voice. "Skunk. A dog got hit by a skunk." His eyes burned and smarted. He could not see. Knocking over chairs, he and his friend ran to the front porch.

"Smart Mole," said Sam, and dashed through the kitchen door.

"I stink!" Bate bellowed from the front porch. Sam

clutched the eyas box. Bate roared on. "I'm going for a can of tomato juice to wash in."

Sam didn't expect that. Bate was stumbling toward the kitchen. Sam was trapped. He put down the eyases. A big box for firewood stood near him, so he opened the lid. The box, as he had hoped, was empty. Into it he went—one second late. Bate was in the kitchen. Sam crossed his fingers in the darkness, hoping Bate's eyes were burning too much to have seen him. He sat perfectly still.

"You're under arrest!" Sam heard a new voice say. "You are stealing falcons." Sam lifted the lid high enough to see not one but two police officers in the doorway. They were facing Bate.

"Where is Skri?" one of the officers asked.

"I didn't steal those birds," Bate said. "The guy you are looking for is in that box. I came in to look around this famous lodge. I found him here with two falcons." He rubbed his smarting eyes. The officers rubbed their eyes, and Sam pushed up the lid of the wood box and stood up.

"Who are you?" an officer asked in surprise.

"Sam Gribley. I live down by Delhi. I came here to get these two chicks and bring them back to their mother. She is nesting near my house."

"That's a likely story," said the other officer.

"He lies," snarled Bate, backing toward his gun on the

sink drain board. In the din of the accusations, a third man entered the kitchen. Sam breathed a sigh of relief. There, in his camouflaged fatigues and hiking boots, was Sean Conklin, the conservation officer of Albany County. He and Sam had tracked down Bate, who, posing as Leon Longbridge, had stolen Frightful from Sam. Sean Conklin would speak up for him. He would let him take the eyases home to Frightful. Sam climbed out of the box, smiling from ear to ear.

Off in the distance Sam heard a car door slam.

"That's Skri," Sam said, "the Arab agent. He's getting away in the pickup."

"Don't worry, Sam," Sean Conklin said. "He won't get away. My assistant, Henry Ryan, removed the spark plugs from the truck."

One of the police officers snapped handcuffs on Bate.

"Let me out of here," Bate snarled. "I'm no thief. I'm a citizen."

"You're no thief, all right," Sam said. "You are worse than that. You're a traitor—an environmental traitor. These little falcons belong to North America."

"I'm a citizen," Bate said, his face growing red with anger.

"Yes, you are," said the officer, "but that doesn't give you the right to sell endangered species. Let's go see the judge." He steered him to the door.

Bate looked back over his shoulder. "I stink," he said. "Can't I even get some tomato juice?"

"I can't smell you anymore," the police officer said. "That's the best part of skunk spray. After a short while, you can't smell yourself—or anyone else who's been doused in it." He chuckled. "But wait till I get home to my wife!"

Sam sniffed himself. He did indeed think he smelled clean. The police officer was right. He sniffed again, then picked up one of the little eyases.

"Hello," he said to the bright-eyed bird, now showing the tips of his wing feathers. "Want to go home to your mom?"

Blue Bill looked at Sam and sat very still, eyes wide.

"He likes you. He sits still even if you do smell," said Sean.

"I wish that were true," said Sam, stroking the downy head. "But the truth is birds can't smell much. He's just scared."

Henry Ryan came in the back door.

"Those two are on their way to jail again," he said, and grinned happily. "This time I hope the judge keeps them there."

Sam picked up the eyas box.

"I'll feed the little birds," he said. "They're restless. They're getting hungry. Then I'll take them home."

"I'm afraid you can't do that," said Ryan.

"Why not?" Sam was astonished.

"You're not a licensed falconer."

"But . . . these are wild birds."

"Not now. They've been registered in Albany. These two little birds are quite famous and are under the protection of the United States government."

"Who is going to raise them?" Sam asked. "They'll never fly free if people raise them."

"A falconer near Delhi is going to raise them—Perry Knowlton. He'll hack them back to the wild. They can learn to be free."

Sam shook his head. He had never heard of Perry Knowlton. He leaned over the box and whispered in falcon talk to the little birds.

"You really should give them to me," he said.

"And why should I do that?" Henry asked.

"I have their mother," Sam said. "She nests in a box at my home on the mountaintop. And she is free."

"Are you kidding?" Henry asked. "Tell me." Sam told Sean Conklin and Henry Ryan the story of Frightful and the Delhi Bridge.

"You say the third chick's in a nest box on your property and its parents are taking care of it?" Henry asked in disbelief.

"Yes," Sam answered. "Frightful would take the little

eyases right back. And that's the best thing for everyone."

"It is," said Henry, "but we can't do that. Too much red tape. The eyases would be grandparents by the time we got through all the bureaucratic loops."

"With every day that passes, they're more deeply imprinted on people," Sam said. "They need their own kind."

"I know that," said Henry. "But we can't turn them over to you."

Mole came into the kitchen. His eyes were still smarting from the direct skunk hit. He sought comfort from Sam.

"Get that dog out of here," said Sean Conklin. "He smells terrible."

"I don't smell him," said Ryan.

"I'm going out on the porch," said Sean, and departed. Ryan followed.

Blue Bill gave a hunger cry. Sam found falcon food in the old refigerator, picked up the eyas box, and went out to the porch.

Mole wagged his tail and trotted after him.

"Stay," Sam said. "And I mean stay right here. I'm going to try once more to get the little eyases. I have one more trick up my sleeve." Mole hung his head, put his tail between his legs, and sat down.

On the porch, Sam and Henry each fed a little falcon, then rocked back on their heels and looked at them.

"Suppose," Sam said slowly and deliberately, "you two had to go to town. And when you got back, the eyases had disappeared?"

"I'd be fired," Henry answered promptly. "And I've got two kids."

"You know we can't do that, Sam," Sean Conklin said.

"Okay," Sam agreed. "But I really don't understand. Everyone wants to save the peregrines, but no one will do what it takes to save them—from stopping work on a bridge to returning chicks to their parents."

He leaned over the eyases, who were now back in their box, full and sleepy.

"Pssst," he squeaked through his tightened lips. "Psst."

The downy birds lifted their heads and turned their huge black eyes upon him. "Creee, creee, creee," he cried, imitating Frightful. The eyases screamed the mother recognition call. Sam touched them gently on the beaks. Then he stood up.

Sean and Henry stared at each other. They had just seen a boy who could talk to peregrine eyases. They knew he was the one person in the world who should have the little birds. And they knew there was no way they could arrange this.

Sam backed down the steps, found his pack in the hemlock grove, and whistled for Mole. Together, they crossed the field in the direction of the mountains.

The two men saw them stride along.

"I think we should have gone to town." Henry said.

"We're not free to do anything but what we did," Sean answered, watching with no little longing the young man who walked to his own inner music.

IN WHICH

Frightful and Oksi Run the Show

The sun was held back by rain clouds the morning Frightful saw Sam and Mole come home from their wanderings. Sam whistled hello, but she did not reply. She was concerned with Oksi. This day had dawned cold, Chup was out hunting, and she had to brood the eyas.

Just as Sam and Mole went into the tree house, Chup came home to feed and brood Oksi, and Frightful took off. She sped with the air currents into a thermal that spiraled her high above Delhi. At the top of the warm air bubble, she peeled off and dove straight down. She landed on the cupola of the county courthouse.

Frightful drew herself up tall. The courthouse pigeon flock was winging into sight. She knew each pigeon personally. She knew the healthy and quick on wing. She knew the dumb and the clumsy. And she knew those with the highly contagious pox virus. She selected one of these and struck. The virus died with the bird, and she carried it back to Oksi.

When Frightful returned with food that day, Chup was freed from his nest brooding. Oksi was old enough to be left alone while Frightful hunted. He flew from tall tree to the tallest, spread his wings, and soared far from Frightful's Mountain. He had never been comfortable in the forest. He was a bird of the cliffs, open river valleys, and the bottoms of clouds. Spread-winged, he rode an air current to a cliff in Catskill Park, a three-minute falcon flight from Oksi. He was still concerned about her.

While Sam and Mole were away, Oksi had changed. The tips of her flight feathers had grown in, and she could stand and walk. She jumped on leaves that blew into the box and watched every bird that flew past. But the greatest change of all was that she jabbed a foot at Frightful when she came into the box with food.

Chup returned to the box one day to find no food at the aerie. He flew down to the river and brought back a duck. Alighting on the box, he was met by Oksi's two yellow feet and black talons. He left the food and took off.

As she grew and changed, the wooden box intrigued Oksi. It was far different from her first home. It did not look out on a vast landscape, but on a hemlock forest. From it she did not see ducks, but frogs and songbirds. The winds around her did not jet, but swirled and bumped.

Instinctively she disliked it, but because her parents fed her here, she became accustomed to it.

Sam would sit at his table at mealtimes and watch Oksi. He knew the box in the forest was all wrong for a peregrine, and so he would wonder what would happen when it came time for her to pick her own nesting site. Would she choose a cliff, a bridge—or, he mused almost longingly, would she pick a beautiful hemlock forest like this? Was she imprinted on Frightful's Mountain?

He was watching Oksi through the binocs one evening when Jessie Coon James came up to him and begged for a handout. Sam laughed and gave her his leftover rabbit stew. Ordinarily he gave it to Mole, but Mole was chasing a fox, and that could take all night. Jessie ate voraciously, then climbed the old hemlock and draped herself over a limb. She closed her eyes.

"Are you sleeping out tonight, Jessie?" Sam asked. "That's a good idea. Think I will, too. It's a balmy night."

A breeze rocked Jessie on her willowy limb.

Sam spread his deerskin sleeping bag on the big stone table and, after completing his chores and writing in his journal, he lay down and watched the stars come out.

Sam listened to the night sounds. A screech owl awoke and called, the barred owl by the mill house hooted, and from far away, he heard the lugubrious voice of Mole reporting his progress in a game of "catch the fox," a game both animals thoroughly enjoyed. After Mole found the scent and began the chase, the fox took great pleasure in tricking him. When Mole got too close, the fox would splash into a stream and wash away his trail, or he would sit in a scented wintergreen patch and watch Mole run right past him. Sometimes he fooled Mole by running the tops of fences or turning around and going back over his own trail. Before dawn, they both understood, the game ended. The fox would slip into his den, and Mole would go home, panting happily.

This night it was Jessie Coon James who had the game

plan. When Sam was asleep, she stole down the tree and circled Baron Weasel's den. Moving quietly, she swam across the millpond to the sluice and climbed up the wall. The shale bricks made perfect hand- and footholds.

She was headed for the roof but was stopped by the overhang. She backed down and tried climbing the down-mountain side of the mill house. Again she was turned back by the overhang.

While she puzzled, Oksi slept, Frightful slept, Sam slept, and Mole ran the top of an old stone fence, following the fox.

Jessie Coon James was not defeated. She walked to the up-mountain side of the mill house. She climbed again, and this time she reached the stovepipe. It was metal and slippery but was braced with steel bands. She caught a band with one front claw and was able to grab the overhang with her hind feet and, scratching hard on the shakes, pull herself up onto the roof.

Oksi awoke. It was dark. She could not see, but she could hear. Something was coming her way. She felt fear for the first time and backed into the corner of the box.

Jessie could see as well in the dark as she could in daylight. She approached the box, hooked eight front claws onto the rim board, and pulled herself in.

Oksi *kakak*-ed, threw up both feet, and sank her talons into the enemy. Jessie yiped a bloodcurdling scream, jumped back, fell, and slid down the roof, clutching with her claws.

Frightful awoke. Oksi was in trouble. She heard but could not see. She sat still.

Sam awoke. He heard Oksi screaming and dashed to the mill house just as Jessie came tumbling down the roof. Sam caught her before she fell.

Jessie's snarls so alarmed Frightful that, despite the darkness, she flew for the nest box. She struck the mill-house roof with a crash, spread out her wings, and lay still.

Sam saw her hit. He climbed to the roof and, taking a grip on the wooden shakes with one hand, grabbed Frightful by both feet with the other. She hung head-down quietly as Sam thrust her into the box. He climbed to the ground and waited.

With Oksi beside her, Frightful shook out her feathers and sat quietly. Oksi did not jab her.

Sam listened. No sounds of distress came from the box.

"Phew," he said, and was about to step on Jessie in the dark when she snarled.

"Jessie, what do I do now?" he asked the raccoon in exasperation. "No matter where I put Frightful and Oksi, in a tree or on a roof, you can get to them."

A silent gray missile sped out of the forest.

The barred owl hit Jessie a one-footed blow on the shoulder and flew up to strike again.

Sam picked up the stunned raccoon. The owl dove at them both. Sam ducked and ran up the hill and into his tree home. He put Jessie on the floor and lit the wick in a turtle shell filled with deer fat.

Light filled the warm interior of the old tree. It shone on the clay fireplace Sam had built from riverside clay. It lit up Frightful's falcon hood on a shelf and threw light on a stack of library books. Sam was preparing to take the high-school equivalency test.

He moved the turtle-shell lamp close to Jessie.

"You've got a mean slash on your shoulder, Jess," he said, then took out his knife and began cutting away the fur from the wound.

"That was Frightful's chick you were trying to eat," he said. "You like Frightful, remember? You never once attacked her, and she never once attacked you.

"You've got to be friends again." He bandaged the wound with sphagnum moss and strips of deer hide. Jessie lay in shock.

Sam talked on, feeling totally inadequate. Telling a falcon and a raccoon to be best friends was almost impossible.

But Jessie had already gotten the peace message. Not from Sam, but from the birds of prey. They had spoken clearly. The territory around the mill house, at the risk of death, belonged to the owls at night and the falcons by day.

Sam stopped talking and picked up his bandaged friend.

He carried her to Alice's tree house to recover out of sight of the birds of prey.

As soon as the sun came up, Frightful left Oksi and flew to the big hemlock. Undaunted by the night's scare, Oksi stood up and watched the awakening birds. She was absolutely intrigued by them at this time in her life and remembered every pattern of the flight of each species.

Suddenly she saw Sam's head coming over the edge of the mill-house roof. She lowered her whole body and ran at him.

"Kak, kak, kak," Oksi warned, and jabbed out a foot.

Frightful flew down from the tree and landed on the top of the box. She looked at Sam, who had reached the box.

"Terrible night, wasn't it, old girl?" he said. "Well, I'm going to fix things. I'm going to get a tall pipe and have Bando solder a metal plate to it. I'll fasten your box to the plate and erect it in the open, where a peregrine aerie ought to be.

"No raccoon can climb a steel pipe," he said, "and your eyas will be safe until she can fly."

"Kak, kak, kak, kak, kak, kak," Oksi screamed, and attacked Sam. When she thrust out her feet, he grabbed them and quickly hooded her.

"Jessie Coon James is laid up," he said to Frightful, "but

not the barred owl—and he can, and will, strike by day. I'm taking your eyas to our tree until the pole's ready."

Frightful called "creee" once. She did not call Sam by his falcon name.

"You are getting wilder, Frightful," he said. "The bond between us is breaking down. That's good. Good for you, sad for me."

Sam made Oksi comfortable inside the tree, then took the trail to Mrs. Strawberry's farm and her collection of pipes and lumber and wheels and scraps of metal.

On the way home he asked Bando for help, and before the sun set, they had put Oksi, unhooded, into the nest box and erected pole, box, and her in the clearing by the millpond. The box now had a porch, where Frightful could drop food without getting jabbed.

They stood back and admired their work.

"It's getting late," Sam said when the job was done. "Aren't you worried about Zella?"

"No," Bando said. "I've got a little gadget in my pocket called a cell phone. Zella will call if she feels any contractions."

"Wow," said Sam, remarking on Zella and the telephone.

Oksi walked out on the porch and *kakak*-ed angrily.

"Neat bird," said Bando, grinning.

"She really is," Sam said, and smiled broadly.

"She does seem a little accident-prone," Bando remarked. "It's been one crisis after another for that bird."

"Yeah," Sam mused. "Only three out of ten birds live long enough to raise their own young."

"Seems," Bando said, "she must be one of those three. She's somehow survived all the hazards of her first forty days."

Sam nodded as he gripped the pole to see if it was firmly planted.

"I'd like to see a raccoon scale that," he said.

"Looks Jessie-proof to me," said Bando.

"Do you realize this is the little eyas's fourth nest site?" Sam said. "I keep wondering what kind of nest she will choose when she grows up and looks for an aerie. She might be a Gypsy nester."

"That's proper," Bando said. "After all, she is *Falco peregrinus*, the pilgrim falcon." They exchanged serious glances. They knew it was important to show this eyas a peregrine's world, and they weren't sure they had done that.

Oksi was oblivious to this chatter. She had her own agenda with her world, and Frightful was the first to discover it.

The very next day Frightful landed on the aerie porch. She was leaning over to pluck a pigeon when Oksi charged her, beak open, feathers raised. She hit her full force. Frightful jumped onto her wings, left the food, and flew to the top of the ancient hemlock.

She shook out her ruffled feathers. Oksi had graduated from grammar school.

From that moment on, Frightful fed her not in the box, but on the wing. She dropped food onto the hacking porch and sped away. She did not perch in the hemlock to chaperone Oksi anymore, but flew over the mountain to the cupola on the Delhi courthouse. There she kept the pigeons of Delhi from spreading disease.

One morning she recognized Leon Longbridge standing on the sidewalk. With him were two children. She kept them in the corner of her eye while she watched the pigeons.

"That *is* our falcon," Leon Longbridge said, focusing his binoculars on Frightful. He grinned and handed the field glasses to Molly.

"How do you know?" Molly asked.

"She has a very dark, almost black, head," he said, "and her eyes are quite large—larger than most peregrines'. When you watch birds long enough, you see their differences. She's our bird, all right." He smiled but did not tell the kids that he had seen the Delhi falcon feeding the third chick in a box on Sam Gribley's mountain.

"Hey," exclaimed Molly. "She sure is our bird. She has little heart-shaped black spots on her breast feathers. I looked at them a million times from my bedroom window."

"You're a good observer," Leon said. Molly looked pleased and passed the glasses to José as Hughie Smith joined them on his way to his drumming lessons. Molly pointed out Frightful to him.

"Neat," he said, and looked up at the conservation officer. "Mr. Longbridge, when can we visit our chicks at Perry Knowlton's?"

"In about two weeks," Leon replied. "He doesn't want them to get comfortable with people while they're young. He's keeping them as wild as possible. He put them with a breeding pair that had only one eyas, and they've been taking care of them. They just might forget their early nurturing by people and become wild."

"I hope so," said Molly.

Leon went on, "Perry said I could bring you all over when he hacks the birds. They'll fly if they are afraid of you—and that's what we want them to do."

Frightful, who was tipping her head now and then to focus on Leon Longbridge and the kids, also had an eye on the courthouse pigeons. When they fanned out and came back together in a silvery knot, she dropped from the cupola, scattered them, and, reaching down with one golden foot, picked up the dumb bird who was flying the wrong way.

Frightful carried the food up over the West Branch of the Delaware.

"Where's she going?" Hughie asked.

"Let's find out," José piped. "Can we follow her, Mr. Longbridge? You're real good at that."

"I don't think we should," Leon answered. "We've given her enough trouble. Don't you think she needs some privacy?"

"Yes," said Molly emphatically, "or she won't come back next year. Peregrine falcons like privacy."

So they stood on the street and watched Frightful until she was too far away to see, which was in mere seconds.

Suddenly Leon Longbridge put his glasses to his eyes and focused them overhead.

"Look! There's her mate," he exclaimed excitedly.

"Cool," said Hughie. "Maybe they'll nest again. It's not too late, is it?"

"I'm afraid it is," Leon Longbridge said. "The tiercel is roaming away from the aerie. That means he's done nesting."

"What do we do now?" complained José. "We can't see the chicks, we can't follow the falcon—"

"There are some transformers up the valley, where our falcon went," said Molly.

"Oh," said Hughie. "Back to letter writing. Okay, I'm getting good at that."

Frightful flew high over one of the transformers Molly was speaking of. She found an updraft on the side of her mountain and rode it without beating a wing. She tipped and sideslipped around the big tree and dropped the pigeon. The bird hit the porch, bounced, and went over the edge. Oksi jumped for it, spread her wings, and was flying. She flapped, shot ahead, and crashed into the ancient hemlock. Grabbing at limbs with her feet, she fell several yards before she got a good grip and flapped herself upright.

Oksi saw the bird. It lay on the ground by Baron Weasel's door. She was very hungry. She dropped down on it, clutched it, then flapped her wings to get airborne. Beating them hard, she skimmed forward but could not get off the ground. At the edge of the millpond she stopped and looked behind her. She had lost the bird.

A bullfrog moved; she thrust out a foot and snagged it. This was not her kind of food, and she let it go. She realized she was on the ground and became nervous. She opened her wings. There was no breeze to give her lift. Frightful's Mountain was a poor place to get airborne. She ran—wings open, pantaloons fluttering—and jumped up onto the stone table.

She sensed a silence around her. Mole was asleep on Sam's bed in the tree. Jessie was down at Peaks Brook. Baron Weasel was in his burrow. The barred owl was perched on a limb halfway down Frightful's Mountain. Only Sam was watching, and he was inside the mill house.

"Accident-prone Oksi," he said to himself. "She's going to get killed if she stays out in the open like that.

"I should grab her feet and toss her onto a wind. No,

that's not right. She's going to have to find out for herself."
He put his elbows on the windowsill. "It's sure terrible," he
mused, "to be a parent knowing that there are eagles and
goshawks lurking everywhere in these mountains."

Sam stood still and watched. Oksi remained on the
table. She was uncomfortable there. Once more she spread
her wings and once more she got no lift. There was no wind
to help her fly.

Mole woke up, smelled Oksi, and pushed open the
deerskin door. His nose directed his eyes, and he ran at her
as he ran at pheasants to flush them up.

He never reached her. Frightful dropped from the sky
and hit Mole with the force of a jackhammer. He yiped and
rolled into the millpond, stunned. His head went under,
and he gulped water.

Terrified, Oksi beat her wings with all her strength and
flew. She flew above Sam, who had waded into the
millpond to save Mole. She came to rest on the mill-house
roof.

Sam pulled the drowning dog to shore.

"Your mouth's too big for mouth-to-mouth resuscita-
tion," he said. "I'll try the Heimlich maneuver." He
pressed down on Mole's chest, then let go. Mole spluttered
and breathed.

He rolled his eyes at Sam.

"Frightful got you," he said. "You can't mess with her

eyas. She's a winged lioness." He helped Mole to his feet. "You and I had just better stay in the hemlock tree until Frightful gets this kid on wing and out of here, or someone is going to get killed."

He helped Mole, who was dripping and coughing, up the slope and into the hemlock. Mole lay down on the floor. After a short while, he breathed normally and thumped his tail.

The talon cut on his head was bleeding profusely. Sam washed it with cold water, saw it was not severe, and patched it with jewelweed leaves to stop the flow of blood. Then he gave Mole a deer bone for consolation and went to his desk. He opened a book.

"As long as we're stuck here," he said, "you might as well learn something. I'll read to you."

He began:

" 'With his first trip to France in 1781, a five-year period began in which Thomas Paine used his skills to work more openly on behalf of the United States to insure that his liberal-republican ideals were implemented.' "

He glanced at Mole. The dog's eyes were closed. "We're on page one hundred thirty-one in Jack Fruchtman Jr.'s book called *Thomas Paine*," he said.

Mole opened his eyes and thumped his tail. Sam went on reading.

IN WHICH

Frightful Feels the Call to the Sky

Atop the mill house, Oksi turned her head almost all the way around in one direction and then the other. She saw trees, boulders, the millpond, and, high above them, a bright glimpse of blue sky. The sky captivated her. She sensed she should be there. She flapped her wings. Nothing happened. The air was still. No wind gave her lift. She closed her wings to her body and flicked her tail in frustration. She needed to be in that sky.

Frightful watched Oksi from Sam's tree. Her eyas had taken her first flight. She was no longer a nestling but a fledgling, a flying member of bird royalty—the family Falconidae. But Frightful was not about to join Chup wandering free on wing. She had still another duty—to provide food until Oksi could catch her own.

Oksi's mood changed from frustration to curiosity. She turned her head almost upside down to focus on a twisting leaf, a flying beetle, and a bird. Birds excited her. She lifted her wings to chase, thought better of it, and folded them to her sides.

Eventually she grew tired and put her beak in the feathers between her shoulders to sleep. The afternoon shadows lengthened and turned purple-blue. Up in the big tree, Frightful closed her eyes. From time to time she opened them and checked on Oksi.

Sam read on. Mole chewed on the deer bone.

Suddenly—"Sam, where are you?"

Bando was running toward the big tree, waving his arms. Oksi awakened and flapped her wings. A gust of wind rushed under them and lifted her off the roof. In seconds she was above the hemlock grove, on her way—somewhere.

Sam saw Oksi soaring to independence at the same time he heard Bando shout. "It's a girl! It's a girl! Her name is Samantha."

"Samantha?" Sam said, and Oksi was forgotten. "Who named her that?"

"Zella," said Bando as he caught his breath from running.

Sam couldn't speak.

"Now we have a son and a daughter," Bando said, putting his hand on Sam's shoulder. "Those are Zella's words."

Sam ran his fingers through his hair, trying to take in the wonder of having a namesake.

"I've got to get back to the hospital," Bando said. "I'll pick up my surprise for Zella and Samantha." He winked. "Think she'll like it?"

Sam still could not speak.

Bando's blue eyes shone under his dark eyebrows and prematurely white hair. His face crinkled around a big smile. He waited for Sam to say something, realized he was overwhelmed, and hurried off to the mill house.

"Samantha," Sam finally said as his friend of the forest and wilderness left the mill house, carrying on his head the exquisite wild-cherry rocking chair he had been working on for eight months.

"Samantha," Sam whispered to himself. "I have a new friend."

Frightful did not hear the excitement. Oksi had disappeared over the mountain, and she was speeding to catch up with her daughter. She finally took the lead and steered to Sam's meadow. She alighted on the limb of an oak tree. Oksi landed on a hickory stub.

Frightful scanned the meadow. Oksi scanned it, too.

A rabbit jumped. Instinctively Oksi dropped from her perch. She missed. She hit where the rabbit had been, not where it would be by the time she struck. The rabbit dove into a patch of greenbrier and Oksi flew back to her perch.

While she sat waiting for something else to run, Frightful flew back to the courthouse. She returned in the late afternoon but brought no food. Oksi, who had still not caught anything, ravenously attacked her mother.

Frightful dodged, climbed swiftly, and sped back to the cupola. In the morning she caught a pigeon.

Oksi saw Frightful flying toward her with the food when she was still a long way off. She waited, then attacked. Frightful dropped the pigeon. With a twist, Oksi caught it in the air and returned to the oak tree. She ate rapaciously.

Although she had never been taught this, Frightful was following ancient peregrine instincts. She was hacking her daughter—bringing her food when she could not catch her own.

Four miles away, on the side of Palmer Hill, Perry Knowlton was doing the same thing for Blue Bill and Screamer.

He carried Screamer to the hack board, a food platform on stilts. He had constructed it below his house on the far side of the pond. It was shaded by a tree. To keep predators like Jessie Coon James from climbing it, he had encased the stilts in tin sleeves. Carefully he removed Screamer's jesses and held him high.

Screamer saw the food on the hack board and flew to it. He was hungry. Perry had not fed him for a day to get him ready for this moment.

"So far so good," he said, and went back to the barn for Blue Bill. Perry held him high.

Blue Bill had imprinted on Perry more deeply than Screamer and was perfectly happy to sit on his hand and admire him.

"Go," Perry said, lowering his fist with a quick downward movement that forced Blue Bill to spread his wings. He flapped and he flew, too, but only as far as a tree limb—not to the hack board. There he sat.

"Ah, come on," Perry said. "You've been a mother's boy since I got you. Now, go join your brother and grow up."

Perry picked up the jesses, leashes, and falconry bells he had taken off the birds and walked the short distance to his bird barn. Blue Bill followed and sat on the roof.

"Ho-ho-ho." Perry bellowed the falconer's cry to encourage a bird to hunt.

Blue Bill turned his head upside down and observed the action until Perry opened the bird-barn door and stepped inside. Then he flapped his wings.

A bald eagle riding up the mountain on a rising thermal saw Blue Bill move and circled to strike.

Screamer, on the hack board, saw the shadow above him and instinctively crouched. He extended his neck and pulled his feathers flat. The great eagle, with its six-foot wingspread, did not see him. He was plunging toward Blue Bill.

Blue Bill saw him and shrieked the alarm cry. Perry ran out of the barn followed by Molly, José, Hughie, and Maria.

The eagle struck Blue Bill. Then he saw Perry and sped off. Blue Bill rolled down the roof and fell to the ground. Perry picked him up and put him under his shirt.

"Is he dead, Mr. Knowlton?" Molly asked fearfully.

"No, but plenty scared," Perry said. "His heart's beating as fast as a woodpecker drills. Let's go inside until he calms down."

The fans of the falcons of the Delhi Bridge trooped back into the clean, roomy bird barn and watched with great concern while Perry stroked the terrified falcon to calm him down.

José watched but was more interested in Screamer. He went to the window of the empty owl room.

"The other bird just flew!" he yelled. "He's going toward Bovina."

"Good," said Perry. "He's off."

When Blue Bill recovered his senses, Perry put him into a carrying cage and covered it with a blanket so that he couldn't see and beat his wings to get free.

"Aren't you going to let him go?" asked Hughie.

"Not today," Perry said. "I'll check him for injuries before I try again. After all, a bald eagle hit him."

"He thinks you're his mom, doesn't he?" Molly asked.

"Sort of," said Perry. "Two falcons raised him from about two weeks of age on, but he seems to have been more imprinted on people than his brother. Because of that, I may never be able to set him free."

"Oh, good," said Maria. "Then we can visit him often."

Perry smiled and opened the barn door.

"Hop in my van," he said. "I'll drive you all back to the courthouse."

"Maybe we'll find the other little falcon," José said. "The road goes close to Bovina."

"Oh, no," said Molly. "I hope he didn't go there. There are lots of transformers around Bovina. I found four when we were writing to the utilities company."

"Time to write letters again," said Hughie with a sigh.

Terrified by the eagle, Screamer had flown to an oak tree at the top of Perry's mountain. His fear died quickly, and he calmly looked around.

A flock of starlings swarmed past him, fanning out and coming back together. He found them interesting—they flew, they moved—they were birds. They swooped into the bushes and vanished. A red-tailed hawk soared by. Instinctively Screamer sat still until the hawk was out of sight. Then the starlings came wheeling back.

Screamer flew into their midst. The birds burst apart, exploding in all directions. He climbed high out of their sight. The birds turned and came back, re-forming their flock. One individual flew alone. Screamer bulleted down and picked it out of the air. He was on his way to independence.

That night he slept near the top of a red spruce. In the morning he followed the starlings that were streaming toward Bovina. They came down in a meadow. Screamer landed on a telephone pole, then skimmed the meadow, scaring the starlings into the air. He chased and attacked, but could not catch one.

Remembering Perry's food-laden hack board, he returned to it late in the morning, ate well, and departed. A few miles away, he stopped to rest. Screamer was outside Bovina again.

That same morning Oksi was sitting in Sam's meadow, hunting by sitting up high waiting for something to move. As the hours passed and she saw nothing, she changed her technique. She came down and skimmed over the tops of the knapweed and grasses to scare up the prey. A rat saw her and ran. She dove, missed, and headed back to the oak tree.

A small house sparrow came by, and she chased it. It dropped out of sight. A rabbit darted off through the weeds.

Oksi tail-chased the rabbit. It ran right, then left, right, left, its white tail warning the other rabbits to hide. Oksi chased right, then left, right, left, and speeded up to strike. The rabbit slipped under a pile of brush and was gone. Oksi flew back to the oak tree.

When Frightful returned to Sam's meadow the next day, Oksi chased her down the mountain. They lit on the bridge at Delhi.

Flocks of ducks and shorebirds had migrated down from the Arctic. They were swimming and eating below the two falcons on the West Branch of the Delaware. The ducks fled when they saw the peregrines. Oksi chased a group, missed them all, looped, and came back to the

bridge. She stood tall and alert. The water, the birds, the sky excited her. The open space felt right to her.

Before nightfall she had snatched a mallard duck that was dying from pesticide poisoning. She carried it to a gingerbread platform near the top of Molly's Victorian house. She ate and fell asleep.

In the early morning a "creee" awoke her. Blue Bill was circling the bridge. She recognized him, although more than a month had passed since she had last seen him. She flew to him, and together they rollicked above the bridge, tumbling on air currents that bounced and rippled like water.

Frightful saw Blue Bill and Oksi circling and diving. She flew to them, and the three falcons played on the invisible roller coasters of wind. When Frightful discovered what skilled flyers they were, she led them onto a rising thermal. They ringed upward and upward, wings spread, not flapping, just tipping now and then to keep them going up.

At two thousand feet they saw Chup far below, sitting on his dead limb above the Schoharie aerie.

Chup saw them, but he felt not one iota of paternalism. His duties were over. He was molting his flight feathers and chose to be alone.

For the next week, Frightful watched her offspring eagerly chase the migrating birds but could not share their excitement. She hunted from the cupola by day, and at night she flew back to the one mountain among hundreds, the one tree among millions, and Sam.

Screamer shuttled between Bovina and Perry's hack board for almost a week.

The day José mailed his letter complaining about the utility poles, Screamer came to rest on a transformer on a pole outside Bovina. A wind gusted; he tried to balance, contacted two wires, and fell to the ground. No one was there to pick him up.

Blue Bill and Oksi stayed around the good hunting grounds of Delhi with Frightful. They soared with her out over the countryside, learning to catch rats, mice, and pigeons. They became expert vermin hunters until Blue Bill found a cliff near the Pepacton Reservoir. Here thousands of migrating waterfowl came down to rest on the water. They were easy to catch, and when they moved on, he went with them. His early visual memory of life with Perry was forgotten. He followed the birds. He was not, after all, imprinted.

But Frightful was. She was held captive by her early training with Sam.

One day she watched a flock of doves disappear over the mountains. She followed them for a short distance, then flew back to the cupola on the courthouse. At dawn the next day she returned to her mountain and the nest box on the steel pole.

Sam was opening the mill sluice to start the waterwheel for Bando, now a busy father. He saw a shadow flash over the water and looked up.

"Frightful!" he shouted.

He held up his hand but did not whistle. Frightful hesitated, circled, and then did something she had never done before. She flew down to his hand without hearing Sam's whistle. Alighting as gently as thistledown, she curled under her toes to keep her talons from piercing his bare hand.

"Beautiful bird," Sam said to her. "Why do you honor me with this visit?"

"Creee, creee, creee," she called softly, leaving off the "car-reet" that said "Sam." He studied her. Her new feathers were darker and more lustrous than last year's. Her eyes were more brilliant and wide open. She was breathing regularly, and her breath was sweet.

"You're one healthy and beautiful bird," he said. "I thought you were here because you need me. But you aren't. Why are you here?"

Frightful faced south.

"Ah, that's it? You're leaving. You've come to tell me good-bye."

Slowly he reached out and stroked her gleaming black head.

"Creee, creee," he piped, but Frightful did not respond.

She looked up at the trees that closed off the sky, beat her wings, circled Sam's head, and climbed out of the forest.

"Good-bye," he called, and stopped. "Hey, what are you doing? You're flying the wrong way." Frightful was flying back to Delhi.

As she passed over Molly's house, she saw Oksi returning to her Victorian gingerbread roost for the night. The abundant pigeons in Delhi had kept Oksi from migrating.

As the light dimmed, the young falcon walked into her elaborate room with its curls and spindles and lay down. She got up, stuck her head out into the dusk, and lay down again. Something was happening to her, and she was restless.

The happening was migration. It was full upon the Northern Hemisphere. The shorter hours of sunlight and lowering temperatures were telling millions of birds to go south. The event had begun in mid-August. The loons, geese, ducks, and shorebirds had heard the message from the environment and had left the barrens of Alaska and Canada. A few days later the swallows and swifts felt the change and left the Northeast.

And now Oksi felt it. Kettles of northern peregrine falcons arrived in the valley. They picked out the weak and slow from the flocks of migrating birds and moved south when their prey moved south. The strong and healthy would survive to have strong and healthy offspring. The weak became life and energy for the falcons. Oksi watched, ate, and listened to the earth's atmospheric messages.

Frightful watched the migrating birds. Some flew west, some south; some migrated by day and some by night. She ate well and grew fat, until at last the shortening days and cold air urged her to go.

But the hemlock tree and Sam urged her to stay.

One chilly September morning, Oksi flew above Delhi, circling old haunts—the bridge, the cupola, and Frightful's Mountain. Near Bovina she got onto a thermal and ringed up and up. Spiraling with her was Chup. He peeled off at the top of the warm bubble and shot southward. Oksi peeled off at the top and joined the great North American bird migration. It was mid-September.

From the bridge top, Frightful saw her go. She lowered her body to fly, straightened up, and sat still. An hour later she returned to the hemlock. She bobbed her head up and down and nervously stacked and restacked her tail feathers. She flew back to the bridge. She flew to the cupola. Nothing was right.

In October she returned to Jon Wood's home. Alighting on the corrected transformer pole, she waited for Susan to appear with food. She saw only the boy who took care of the farm when the Woods were gone.

The pigeon cote was noisy, the rat cages were correctly smelly, but all were somehow wrong. She flew over the Schoharie Reservoir where she had weathered a storm. Frightening messages from the rays of the sun told her she was going the wrong way.

She flew back to the one mountain among hundreds, the one tree among millions, and Sam.

Mole was in the tree snoozing on Sam's bed, and Jessie

Coon James was in a hollow, dozing in winter lethargy. Sam and Alice were sitting around a small fire, cracking hickory nuts and putting the meats in clay tureens for the winter.

"Zella named her Samantha," Sam said. "Isn't that nice?"

"I know, I know," replied Alice. "How many times have you told me that? I saw her, and she's too little for such a big name."

"She'll grow up."

"They'll call her Sam, and then what?"

"That's even better," he said.

Alice stuffed a large piece of hickory meat into her mouth.

"Creee, creee, creee, car-reet."

Sam jumped to his feet.

"Alice," he said. "It's Frightful. She's here. She's not going to migrate. What do I do?"

"Call her down and keep her," Alice answered. "She would like that."

"I can't. Since I can't have her, I want her to be a wild peregrine falcon. She must go."

"Does every single, solitary peregrine have to migrate?"

"No," he answered thoughtfully. "There are some who have stayed near New York City all winter because there are so many pigeons. But they are not Frightful. She

must be a one-hundred-percent pure peregrine, sailing
blue skies, journeying to new worlds—and that means she
migrates."

"Oh, Sam," Alice said, then thought a minute. "What
makes birds migrate?"

"A lot of things, but mostly lack of food in the cold
north. They follow the food supply."

"Then don't feed her if you are so anxious for her to be
a pilgrim falcon."

"I'm not going to," he said, stepping back to try to find
Frightful among the branches of the ancient hemlock, but
primarily to keep Alice from seeing his great sadness. He
wanted Frightful to stay with all his heart.

"I'm not going to," he repeated.

I N W H I C H

The Earth Calls Frightful

And then it happened.

Frightful hopped from limb to limb until she
reached the wispy top of the ancient hemlock. She turned
her head slowly as she took a bearing on the sun's rays. She
fixed on a longitude between ninety and seventy degrees.
After many takes, the direction was indelibly printed on her
brain. She pointed her head and body along the invisible

line. She bent her knees and ankles. She lowered her wings.

"Alice," Sam whispered. "Frightful's leaving us!"

"How do you know?"

"Look at her. She has that southward concentration of migrating birds. I've seen it in robins and blackbirds."

Frightful flew. She did not look back.

"But she loves you," Alice cried. "She can't go. She doesn't know what to do without you."

"But she does," said Sam, watching her disappear. "She's flying south.

"Come back in the spring," he called, then added, "I'll be waiting."

Sam climbed the old hemlock, trying to catch one last glimpse of his beloved bird. She was already far away.

She rode the prevailing wind over the familiar mountains and rivers and beyond the Catskills into unknown territory. She did not hesitate or turn back. She memorized the landscape as she flew—forests, rivers, highways, and cities. In one hour she saw the Atlantic Ocean ahead. Its plantless expanse told her it was not the way to go.

She came down on a tor above the Hudson River and perched in an isolated ash tree. A Cooper's hawk and two red-tails were hunting not far away.

Frightful noted the moisture in the air, the clouds, the wind, and the other migrating birds passing overhead.

Blackbirds swarmed over the cattail swamp at the bottom of Hook Mountain.

In the morning the sky was clear and blue. She perched in the top of the ash, waiting for the earth to warm and the wind to rise and carry her on her way.

She took off about nine o'clock.

"Peregrine!" a man on the top of Hook Mountain shouted with gusto. He was seated before a spotting scope.

"That makes forty peregrines for the month," said a woman sitting on a camp stool. She put a check beside "peregrine falcon" in the raptor counting book. The tor top was speckled with men and women who came to Hook Mountain in the autumn to count the birds of prey. Each year these people, like thousands of others, tallied raptors along the four migratory flyways in North America—the Atlantic, Mississippi, Central, and Pacific flyways. They counted because the birds of prey were losing ground in the fight for survival. By comparing their numbers each year, the counters could tell whether or not their efforts to ban pesticides and pass laws protecting the birds were working. The birds of prey were vital to the health of North America.

The people on Hook Mountain cheered when Frightful went over. A peregrine was a thrill to see. The bird had been eliminated by DDT and pesticides in much of the

United States in the forties, fifties, and sixties. Even now it was still a rare sight—a beautiful rare sight.

Frightful's wings cut circles in the wind that sped her southeast toward the ocean. Abreast of New York City, she sensed she was off-course. Her internal compass and the increasing moisture in the air sent her westward. Rough air bounced her back and forth, but she found her longitude again over the New Jersey marshlands.

She dropped down to rest on the post of a duck blind. A shotgun blasted.

She took off, skimmed low over the tops of the sedges until she found a thermal, and rode it, ringing swiftly up, barely moving her wings as it carried her out of the range of the duck hunters' guns.

Soaring, tipping, circling at the top of the thermal was Drum.

"Creee, creee, creee," she called. Her first tiercel eyas answered with nestling talk, "Pseee," then adult talk, "Creee, creee, creee."

They sped out of the thermal together and started down the coast. They flew extremely high, keeping the ocean on their left. Drum had taken this trip last year. He picked smooth winds between towers of clouds as he led Frightful through the sky.

Frightful and Drum and several other birds of prey kept each other in sight. Traveling together, they formed a sky club. Before long they came to know each other and passed on information about the weather and the terrain. The experienced ones knew to come down early before a storm. Others sensed turbulence approaching and took detours around destructive winds.

Over Virginia a sudden gust of dry air pushed Frightful ahead of Drum. She had learned at Delhi that such a wind would be followed by a cold front. She flew faster to keep ahead of it. Six hundred miles from Hook Mountain, she came down on a utility pole on Cape Hatteras. Fifteen minutes later Drum joined her. Dropping out of the sky by twos and ones came the goshawk, the kestrel, the red-tailed, and the sharp-shinned—the bird club. They spread out over the vast wetland.

Frightful looked down on black ducks, mallards, blue-winged teals, plovers, godwits, yellowlegs, sandpipers—all the migrating birds that loved wetlands. At the sight of a peregrine falcon they vanished. Frightful did not chase them. She was looking for pigeons and rats but actually was not very hungry. She was living on her migratory fat. Perched on the pole, she oiled her feathers, which had become dry at the high altitudes. Drum oiled his on the mast of a sailboat that had been dumped in the marsh by a long-ago storm.

In the morning Frightful did not follow Drum southward. The wind was wrong. It was coming from the southeast, bending the trees to the northwest. She recalled the winds that had preceded the storm on the Schoharie Reservoir and flew inland to the little town of Plymouth, North Carolina. She landed on the bell tower of a church. She knew a church tower well, found one of the open windows, and walked in.

Drum had not gone far before he realized the winds were wrong. He back-flipped in the air and came down on a water tupelo tree about three miles from Frightful. The tree had grown great buttresses to support it in storms and in the watery soil.

Frightful in her church and Drum in his tupelo sat quietly through screaming gusts and dead calms. They preened. Frightful watched a duck fly into the reeds and a willet find shelter behind a dense clump of sedge.

The next day the winds were stronger. Lengths of clouds became stringy clusters of gray. Frightful stayed in her church tower, Drum settled closer to the bole of the tupelo tree.

Two nights later, windblown rain began to fall. First in light dribbles, then in gushes. The ducks and geese and herons hunkered down in the sedges and reeds. The warblers had gone inland to the pine forests. They pushed close to the tree trunks. The falcons and hawks sought shelter in forests and buildings. Those that had felt the lowering pressure of the storm, before Frightful and Drum had felt them, had flown west to get around it. They were sleeping in Kentucky and Tennessee.

Around two o'clock, Frightful's church tower vibrated

in the high wind. A shutter was torn from the rectory. It clattered down the street, breaking into splinters. The lights in the town went out. Frightful awoke from time to time, when the wind blew so hard it rang the church bells. She shook off the rain coming horizontally in through the windows, then put her beak into the feathers of her back and went to sleep.

Drum was not as comfortable. His tupelo tree lashed and coiled like a whip in the wind. He crouched, tightening his grip on the limb, and faced into the storm. Hours passed.

Just before dawn, a tidal wave six feet high roared across the marsh. It was seawater that had been lifted up into the center of the hurricane by the low pressure. It hit the base of Drum's tree and rose so fast that Drum was forced to fly. He could not see well, but he knew the direction of the forests. Beating his wet wings, he was carried, rolling and tumbling, low over the marshland. He crashed into a hill of groundsel bushes and wedged his way into their dense center. Then he climbed away from the rising water. Drum went lower into the bushes just as a 110-mile-an-hour wind struck. It ripped off every groundsel leaf, leaving the limbs bare. Gripping with all his strength, Drum faced into the storm, his streamlined body minimizing the wind.

Then came the calm. The eye of the storm passed through Plymouth at about two in the afternoon. Frightful was awakened by an all-encompassing silence. Drum sat still. This was no time to fly. Half awake, half asleep, he waited.

In the morning the eye of the hurricane was off to the north, and the far side of the storm struck the marshland. It was less forceful. The winds blew west now. Frightful stayed in the church tower. Drum stayed in the flooded groundsel bushes. The rain slowed, and the tide receded. By the end of the day the hurricane was off Cape Hatteras, on its way north. The sun came out.

Frightful caught one of several wet rats that had retreated to the church and crawled up to the bell tower. Drum shook the water from his feathers and flew inland. He climbed high, found a brisk wind, and sailed down the coast toward Florida.

Frightful took off around noon. She also climbed high. Although she had never seen the swamps and forests of Georgia and Florida, she sensed their place and recorded them on her visual mind. Navigating with her were members of the bird club. They had weathered the storm in trees and docks inland from the cape. Left behind were gaggles of ducks and geese. They had found their winter destination. The peregrine falcons flew on.

Two days after the storm, Frightful came down in a Florida sable palm and noted her global position again— eighty degrees longitude. She took off and flew over the tip of Florida. The club had dispersed. Each had gone on to its own ancestral wintering grounds. Two new companions joined Frightful, one an older peregrine falcon and the other a young tiercel.

The winds were light, and Frightful had to work hard to keep up her speed in the warm air below the tropic of Cancer.

She stopped overnight in Cuba and flew on the next day.

Immediately she was over the open water with no landmarks. She guided herself by the rays of the sun. When clouds piled up in the late afternoon, she came down on a key off the shore of Belize, caught food, rested, and went on.

She was alone now. She followed her directional line over the Caribbean Sea and caught up with Drum as they were approaching the Isthmus of Panama.

Drum looped in greeting. They flew in tandem to the palms and ficus trees on Barro Colorado Island and came to rest in black mangrove trees. They did not eat. A great urgency drove them on. In the morning they were over the Pacific Ocean, headed for Chile.

The winds changed from smooth glass to bumps. Drum recognized the edge of a tropical storm and turned east.

Frightful flew west. She also recognized the texture of the air and the color of the sky that foretold atmospheric trouble, but she chose to fly around the disturbance. Drum's course took him back to his wintering grounds on the Chilean shore.

Frightful flew for almost an hour to get around the storm before turning south. No land was in sight. She flew on.

In the late afternoon she held her wings straight out to glide and save energy. She dropped closer and closer to the surface of the ocean. She saw no resting place, not even a boat.

She flew all night.

At sunup she was still just above the water, her wings outstretched, gliding to find a badly needed bit of land. All was water.

As she looked and glided, a flock of storm petrels winged by. They wheeled in the orange sunrise. A flock of blue-winged teals flew with them. These were no birds of the ocean. They were birds of the land.

Land was near. Frightful summoned new energy and climbed into the sky. In the distance she saw a green-gray island.

With a last effort, she pumped her wings and flew straight ahead and came down on a *palo santo* tree on Española Island. Birds flew lazily above it. Male frigate birds with bright red balloonlike sacs under their chins cruised the shore. Not three feet from Frightful, seven little black

Darwin cactus finches were busily gleaning food. She waited for them to flee. All birds fled from her. The Darwin finches kept on hopping and eating. They did not know they should beware of predators. Frightful had arrived in the Galápagos Islands, six hundred miles out in the Pacific Ocean, where the birds and reptiles had lived for hundreds of thousands of years, perhaps millions, without predators. They were totally unafraid.

Frightful was unable to chase the friendly birds. They did not fly away from her, and because they did not, she was not inspired to chase them. She was exhausted and hungry amid friendly creatures. She was watching them, growing listless from hunger, when a wheeling flock of sanderlings and whimbrels from the continent flew past. They acted familiarly. They flew together and apart at the sight of a predator, and Frightful dove into their midst. She gave chase and finally ate.

Returning to the *palo santo* tree, she rested not far from a group of Galápagos mockingbirds. They were not as innocent as the little finches. They were attacking everything—iguanas, birds, other mockingbirds, and Frightful herself. They did not know she was a predator, but they did not like any other living thing in their territory. They swooped and dove and pestered. She returned the compliment. She swooped and dove—and they all stayed away.

From her perch she watched young sea lion cubs and

their mothers tumbling on the beach. The huge bulls were in the water. They roared and bellowed when another male came near their harem and offspring.

Something moved at the foot of Frightful's tree. She focused. A three-foot-long land iguana was chewing cactus fruits. His dragonlike spines and thick skin sent a strong message to her. He was not food.

For several hours Frightful bobbed her head and looked from one strange animal to another in this world of ancient survivors.

At sunset, clouds piled up like purple mountains, forecasting rain. Frightful flew to a shelter she had pinpointed on her arrival. She crossed the water to Gardner's Island and alighted on a steep lava cliff of cracks and niches. All were occupied by blue-footed boobies, big birds with startlingly blue feet. They chased her off their properties. She dropped to another shelter and was ushered out by Galápagos penguins. These perky, upright birds had been lost from the ice islands of Antarctica hundreds of thousands of years ago and, unable to swim back, had adjusted to the tropical heat. They cooled off by lifting their wings, panting, and jumping into the icy water.

Frightful left the penguins and blue-footed boobies to their caves and niches and rounded the island, looking for shelter. She came upon another cave on the western cliff, facing the oncoming storm. The cave was scoured by wind, sea, and water, and was deep enough for shelter. She walked into it.

That night a downpour pelted the cliff side. Frightful shook rain from her feathers without awakening. In the morning, bright sunlight turned the roughened water into patches of flashing silver. The clouds were gone. Frightful flew back to Española Island for food.

It was vacation time for peregrines, and Frightful sensed it. She flew for the sheer pleasure of flying. She winged out over the water to be rocked by warm sea winds. She climbed up into storm clouds and rolled out of them into sunshine. She turned loops and spirals.

Each morning for the next two months, she played with the air currents high above her rocky little island, then streaked to her *palo santo* on Española Island. When the daily tourist boats arrived around ten o'clock, she flew back to her island, leaving the sea lions, Darwin finches, marine iguanas—all the original residents—to entertain the people. They did this admirably, since they were totally unafraid of the two-legged mammals. Until three hundred years ago, no humans had come to these isolated islands, and the birds and reptiles had not learned to run from them. Their inherited memories covered one million years without people, and so the birds hopped close to tourists and fishermen. The sea lions did not move when photographers walked among them. Lizards challenged lizards while people

watched, and marine iguanas walked between human feet on their way down the beaches to feed in the sea.

On December 21, the day of the winter solstice, something happened to Frightful.

The image of the one mountain among thousands, the one tree among millions, and the one boy, Sam Gribley, flashed in, then out of her mind.

Three days later she left Gardner's Island. She stopped on Española for a week, eating well and putting on fat for the long flight ahead. She was going home. The sun had changed only a few seconds at the equator, but it was telling her body to migrate.

She pointed her beak south. In New York, shorter days had told her to go south. Here in the tropics the days were now growing shorter, and Frightful pointed her beak the wrong way.

She was ready to take off when a Galápagos hawk landed on a cactus in front of her. His feathers were dark brown, his eyes yellow. He flew into her face. Frightful fell backward, twisted onto her wings, and sped. Two other male Galápagos hawks came after her. They were a family of three males and one female. The males were defending their nest on a cactus not a hundred yards from where Frightful had sat. They all helped one female raise her chicks, each of which had a different father. The hawk family passionately attacked falcons from the north. Having sent Frightful on her way, the three males came after her, but Frightful's tapered falcon wings were faster than their broad hawk wings. She sped to the end of the island and rested on a lava rock.

Frightful was facing north. Suddenly the iron bits in her brain clicked a strong message to her—fly straight on. Her brain was feeling the pull of the earth's magnetic field, slight as it was.

Frightful flew north.

She flew along longitude ninety degrees, the longitude along which the Galápagos Islands lie. After a half hour's flight, she landed on a *palo santo* tree at the top of a dead volcano. She lingered uncertainly among complacent woodpeckers from the north. They confused her. They were busy being home lovers. Their ancient ancestors had found the Galápagos Islands so pleasant that they had not returned north. Frightful might have remained with them had not a flock of pintail ducks come down on the shore below. She chased them. Three left the island, headed north. She followed them, sensing that her inner compass had finally kicked in and was correct.

Frightful and the ducks came to rest on Darwin Island, the last outpost before El Salvador, a thousand miles away. Frightful was now north of the equator, but only about ten miles. She lingered on this bird-rich island to put on more fat.

In early January the sun's message was stronger. The days were several seconds longer—spring was coming to the north. She crouched low, straightened up, and bobbed her head. The one mountain among thousands, the one tree among millions, and the one Sam Gribley were pulling her home. She flew up the Galápagos longitude, headed straight for El Salvador in line for Wisconsin.

For many miles, she flew over the Pacific Ocean with a flock of red-rumped storm petrels. They dove for tiny fish. Around her, gulls screamed and pelicans flapped laboriously. Then the land birds vanished and she saw only birds of the open ocean, the albatrosses and snowy terns. Frightful sensed she was far from food and land.

The sun set orange-red on the ocean, and in seconds it was night. There is no true twilight in the tropics. The stars instantly appeared in the black sky, reflecting their light on a quiet ocean.

Alone in the starlight, Frightful flew on.

She breathed steadily as she followed her internal homing equipment. To save energy, she flapped her wings strongly, then soared for long periods on the errant winds.

She kept going.

In the morning she was on a clockwise wind that was carrying her east. She turned to get back on course when she saw land birds in the distance. She caught up and flew with them. They grew more numerous, then floating seaweed told of land not far ahead. Frightful held her wings outstretched and glided on the wind.

She put her feet down on a coconut palm on Cocos Island.

Sandpipers ran along the beach; gulls screamed and looped through the air. Migrating birds rested and gathered strength for the long flight north.

Frightful rested, then darted around Cocos Island for three days, eating and sleeping and gaining weight. When the sun had added another two minutes to the day, the mountain, the tree, and the boy appeared in her mind. Taking another reading on the sun's rays, feeling the magnetic pull of the earth, she flew north on the fateful ninety-degree line headed for Wisconsin.

Three hundred miles beyond Cocos Island, Frightful knew there was land to the east. She did not see birds or seaweed, but she felt the mass of a continent.

Ignoring the sun, she turned and flew east. After an hour manipulating bumpy winds, she arrived at the Isthmus of Panama.

Frightful flew directly to the mangrove tree on Barro Colorado Island where she had rested in the autumn.

She ate and slept. For three days she stayed on the island, looking northward from time to time, realigning her compass. When the rays of the sun and her magnetic sense lined her up with eighty degrees longitude, she was ready to fly. The one mountain in thousands, the one tree among millions, and Sam were straight ahead.

"Creee, creee, creee."

Drum slammed down beside her.

They exchanged soft noises of recognition, then swooped over the island, chased each other, ate well, and started home.

The trip progressed slowly at first. Frightful and Drum stopped in Cuba for ten days and along the northern coast of Florida for a week. As the days grew longer, they went faster. They lingered in South Carolina for only five days, flew over North Carolina, and came down for a day in Virginia. Cape May, New Jersey, was their next stop. On the narrow peninsula they met hundreds of other raptors going north to their aeries, their nests and scrapes. Frightful barely noticed them. No sooner was she rested than she took off for the one mountain among thousands.

Navigating now by the sight of familiar forests and rivers, she arrived home in three and a half hours and dropped into the one tree among millions.

"Creee, creee, creee, car-reet," Frightful called.

IN WHICH
Destiny Is on Wing

Frightful looked down on a snowy mountain. "Cree," she called softly to her nest box on the raccoon-proof pole. She recognized it under mounds of snow and ice and lifted her feathers in pleasure.

Other familiar objects caught her attention. There were the stone table and log seats. They had been cleared of snow. Baron Weasel's den was still under the rock. The snow around it was stamped with his footprints. The waterwheel was there, but not turning. The millpond was ice. A feeling of contentment settled over Frightful, and she rested from her long journey.

"Creee." Frightful looked up. Drum was overhead. He circled and called for her to follow him.

Frightful sat still. She was where she wanted to be—home with Sam. Drum dove toward her, called again, gave up, and went on. He was eager to get to his aerie in the Adirondack Mountains. On a steep cliff his mate of last year had laid eggs that had broken under her weight. Pesticide chemicals had accumulated in her body and weakened the eggshells. A week later she died from poisons she had accumulated in South America from eating birds that had eaten DDT-sprayed insects. Drum must find another mate this year.

Frightful swooped down onto the nest box. Snow splashed out in all directions. She jumped from the roof to the hacking porch, scattering that pile of snow. Leaning down, she peered into her old nest and walked far back into the cozy box. She picked up a windblown leaf in her beak.

After a long stay there, she flew to the stone table to look for Sam.

The deerskin door of the hemlock tree bumped open. Mole came out. He bounced through the snow, tunneled through deep drifts, surfaced, and ran down the trail.

Frightful flew after him, leaving her wing prints on the snowy table. She was hungry, and Mole, she sensed, was going hunting in the meadow where the rabbits and pheasants lived. She flew ahead of him and waited in the oak tree for him to arrive. He did not appear. Mole was tearing downhill to Mrs. Strawberry's farm for his daily treat from Alice.

A whistle from the mountaintop never reached Frightful's ears, nor did the words, "Frightful! You're back. You left your wing prints on my table! Where are you?"

Sam whistled the three notes that would bring Frightful to him, but she was out of earshot.

When Mole didn't show, she took to the air. Her hunger reminded her of the courthouse cupola and the pigeons. She skimmed down the mountain and followed the river valley to Main Street. Throwing out her yellow feet, she came to a gentle landing on the courthouse cupola.

The pigeon prospects were wonderful. Mrs. Dorst and her daughter, Ms. Sarah Denny, had fed the pigeons so well during the winter that they were already nesting and laying eggs. Without the peregrine falcons to keep them in check, they were so numerous that the courthouse windows and ledges were white with birdlime. Frightful had an endless feast before her.

Her biological clock was ticking rapidly toward nest-scraping time. This put her in a mood to check nest sites. Late in the afternoon she flew to the Delhi Bridge and walked to her old scrape on the girder. She did not remember the noise of last spring, but her visual memory was clear. She recalled trucks shaking the webbing, men on scaffolds and cherry pickers. She flew back to the courthouse. A visual image of the cliffs along the Schoharie was the next site to check. She watched the sky for Chup.

Molly came skipping down Main Street, spotted Frightful sitting erect and dignified on the courthouse cupola, and broke into a run. She dashed into the county courthouse building and found Leon Longbridge working at his desk.

"She's back," Molly cried excitedly. "The peregrine falcon of Delhi is back!"

"Are you sure?" Leon Longbridge was grinning.

"Definitely," Molly said. "Her head is almost pure black. Her breast is rosy white, and she's just beautiful. She's our falcon."

They stood side by side on the sidewalk across the street from the courthouse. Leon focused his binoculars.

"By golly," he said. "You're right. Not only is her head exceptionally black, but she's right in her favorite perching spot."

"Will she nest there?" Molly asked.

"Maybe. Falcons and most other birds come back to their old territories year after year," he said. "Some even return to the same nest sites."

"The bridge?" said Molly. "Will she nest on the bridge?"

"I don't know. Peregrine females are unpredictable."

"She has to. She just has to," said Molly. "That would be so cool."

Frightful cocked her eye and focused on a speck in the sky. She bobbed her head. Chup was speeding like a crossbow along the edge of a cloud. He was a mile away. She waited. He went right over Delhi and the mountain, heading for his cliff in the Schoharie Valley. Frightful was in the air before Leon Longbridge could say another word about female peregrine falcons.

"Chup, chup, chup, chup," the tiercel called. Frightful heard the peregrine love song. She caught up with him and flew at his side. They chased in and out of the misty edge of an ice cloud.

But Frightful felt she was going the wrong way. Her mountain was behind her. She tipped her wings, banked, and started back. The west branch of the Delaware, the town of Delhi, and the one mountain among thousands were where she belonged.

Chup came after her. He looped so appealingly that she looped in response. When she finished the aerial flip, she was flying close behind Chup, back to the cliff above the Schoharie River.

She landed on the ledge where she had helped raise Chup's motherless eyases. Lifting her tail and leveling her body, she walked to the abandoned scrape.

She straightened up—this was not right.

Chup, perched on the ledge of the aerie, watched her carefully. Frightful lifted all her feathers to make herself appear enormous. Chup backed up. The female peregrine was the power of spring. He bowed to her.

Frightful flew off. Chup followed her. Above Jon Wood's house, she located the tall silo and circled it. It had ledges for a scrape, and food abounded here. She landed just under the roof. Chup came down beside her. He did not like what he saw and flew back toward his cliff.

Frightful also found the spot not to her liking, but she

did not return with Chup. She flew directly to her mountain and landed on the wooden box. After a long wait, Chup joined her. She was the falcon. She made the nesting decisions.

Chup came as far as the ancient hemlock and stopped. He would go no farther. A nest box on a pole in a forest was totally wrong. He called to her and flew back to the Delhi Bridge. The span was relatively quiet. Sitting high above a river of ducks and waterfowl, Chup felt better. He waited for Frightful.

Atop the nest box, Frightful sat still—resolute. Presently she heard the voices of Sam and Alice as they came up the snowy trail from Mrs. Strawberry's farm. She fluffed her feathers. They brought pleasure to her.

"Well, what do you think, Sam?" Alice asked. "Isn't that exciting?"

"Yes, yes, it is," he answered. "I really would like to manage Mrs. Strawberry's farm for her."

"Not manage," Alice said. "She wants to give it to us when you're of age."

"We'll see about that," Sam said. "It should be yours. You've brought her prosperity with your Crystal and her Poland piglet offspring. And I have my own farm—my wilderness."

"I need your help," Alice said. "I can take care of the pigs, but not the fields."

Alice was quiet while they went on all fours up an icy hill.

"Besides," she at last said, "Dad and Mom and the kids would like the old farmhouse."

"They sure would!" Sam chuckled. "If Dad didn't have to plow rocks like he did up here, he would be happy all right." He thought a minute.

"You know, Alice," he said, "I have come to realize that I am a farmer already."

"You are," Alice said. "And so another farm would be perfect for you."

He tilted his head wistfully as he thought out loud.

"I am a farmer of wild foods—wild rabbits and pheasants, wild cattails and hickory nuts and walnuts." He was quiet, then went on.

"I sowed the abandoned field with plants the birds like and clover the rabbits like, and planted the clearings in the forest with wild bulbs and mountain lettuce. I've kinda made the Gribley farm produce what it is best suited for—wild crops."

"You sure did that," Alice said. "But with the Strawberry farm you can also have barbecued spareribs, and bread from the wheat crop."

The trail ended, and they walked to the root cellar. Sam brushed the snow off the door and thought about the evening's menu.

"Creee, creee, creee, car-reet."

He spun on his heel.

"Frightful!"

Sam whistled the three notes that had once brought her to his fist. She did not respond.

"You've been on a long trip, haven't you?" he said. "Your life is different now—all but your nest. You must remember raising Oksi here."

Frightful peered at him.

"You're one gorgeous falcon," he said. "Will you stay?"

"Oh, she has to," Alice said.

Still addressing Frightful, Sam went on, "Frightful, stay with me. I will manage Mrs. Strawberry's farm so you will never go hungry. I know how to increase the numbers of quail and pheasants and rabbits. Or do you hunt ducks and waterfowl now? I can increase their numbers, too. Come live with me on my wilderness farm."

Frightful hopped to the hacking porch.

"She must stay," said Alice, clenching her hands in excitement. "We'll have little eyases. They'll be free. No conservation officer can take them away."

"Chup, chup, chup."

"Creee, creee, creee," Frightful answered.

Chup was circling Frightful's Mountain.

She called to him. Chup circled in the sky once more.

He looped and flew upside down. He called the love song of the peregrine falcon.

Frightful hopped to the porch and took off.

She sped up into the cloud where Chup was cutting arcs and circles. She looped and spiraled.

In tandem they flew down the river valley. Near Delhi, Frightful took the lead. She went down Main Street, sped over Elm Street, and landed on the cupola of the court-house.

She scratched away the windblown leaves with her saffron-yellow feet and sat down.

She was home.

Chup knew it. He bowed to his mate.

Destiny's new life had begun.

A bowlike speck appeared over Frightful's Mountain. It grew larger and larger as it came toward earth. An instant later, Sam heard wind whistling through wing feathers. He looked up. Oksi bulleted down from the sky and alighted on the wooden box.

She called for a mate.

Afterword

If you go to Delhi, New York, you will not find the bowstring truss bridge over the West Bank of the Delaware River. I am a novelist, and I put it there for Frightful. A peregrine needs a high aerie with a beautiful view. However, nearby in the mountains you might find Jon and Susan Wood and Perry Knowlton. They are falconers who are urging the utility companies to make a simple adjustment on their transformers to save birds of prey. I invented their conversations and some of the incidents in which they take part, but I have truthfully represented their lives and work and their love of our birds of prey. They read the manuscript and agreed to be characters in this tale.

Heinz Meng is also a real person. He raised the first peregrine falcons in captivity and hacked them to the wild when everyone said it couldn't be done. A warm and extraordinary man, he asks no praise. His reward is sharing his knowledge with those who would help the peregrine falcons. Dr. Meng is a professor at State University of New York at New Paltz.

All the other characters are fictitious. The mountains are not. Ira Macintosh, who has climbed and camped in these beautiful forests, has checked out every name and slope for me.

Finally, this is also true: Peregrines nested on the Kingston-Rhinecliff Bridge that spans the Hudson River in New York State. When repairs began, no authority would stop the work to protect the endangered birds. Eventually the U.S. Fish and Wildlife Service moved the eyases, and the peregrines did get their young on wing. But the bridge-repair work never stopped for even a day.

JEAN CRAIGHEAD GEORGE